13.05

AN AVALON ROMANCE

OUT OF THE SHADOWS
Sheryl Leonard

The last thing Wendy needed was another man to break her heart.

Recovering from her fiancé's betrayal in the remote Pacific coastal village of Shadow Ridge, Wendy Hunt is not looking for romance. Coming on the heels of her father's abandonment, this latest heartbreak has convinced her that life is less painful without love. Wendy intends to live a man-free life from now on. Of course, she never reckoned on meeting Eric Tremaine.

Eric has arrived in town from Seattle to search for his estranged brother, Scott, whose last known address was in Shadow Ridge. When Eric elicits Wendy's help, she finds she is fighting her growing attraction to him. She only hopes he leaves before he steals her heart completely.

As Eric and Wendy search for Scott, they face more than shifty art dealers and Canadian Mounties with secrets; they must also confront some ghosts of past hurts before they can step out of the shadows and love again.

OUT OF
THE SHADOWS

•

Sheryl Leonard

AVALON BOOKS

NEW YORK

Published by Avalon Books,
an imprint of Thomas Bouregy & Co., Inc.
160 Madison Avenue, New York, NY 10016

Library of Congress Cataloging-in-Publication Data

Leonard, Sheryl.
   Out of the shadows / Sheryl Leonard.
      p. cm.
   ISBN 978-0-8034-7795-7 (acid-free paper)   1. Nurses—
Fiction.   2. Missing persons—Fiction.   3. British
Columbia—Fiction.   I. Title.
   PR9199.4.L462O98 2010
   813'.6—dc22

                                          2010018146

PRINTED IN THE UNITED STATES OF AMERICA
ON ACID-FREE PAPER
BY HADDON CRAFTSMEN, BLOOMSBURG, PENNSYLVANIA

To the One who knows
me best and loves me
more than I deserve

Chapter One

Wendy Hunt picked up her pace, eager to get back to the nurses' residence. She had underestimated two things: the length of time the home visit would take, and the dense fog that would roll in off the bay and conceal the moonlight. On a country road without street lamps, the moon and stars were all the light she had to guide her after dark. She pulled her coat tightly around her and walked as fast as the muddy road allowed.

Her present destination, Shadow Ridge, lay twenty minutes straight ahead. Since fleeing Vancouver with her heart and pride in tatters, Wendy had found refuge and a new life five hundred kilometers north in this remote fishing village, where the small hospital had welcomed her nursing skills with desperate, open arms.

Two lights suddenly pierced the fog, creating a surreal glow from behind her. A blast of honking warned her that a vehicle was coming up fast. Instinctively, she sprang to the shoulder but overshot the width. She slid down the embankment into a deep trough, landing with a thump on her rear end in a puddle of icy water.

"Yikes!" she yelped, as cold wetness seeped through her coat and jeans. A moment ago she had been dry, upright, and walking along the road back to the nurses' residence; now she was sitting in mud, a mess.

"No good deed goes unpunished," she muttered, and she scrambled to her feet, unhurt. She wiped her hands on her coat, not removing mud from her hands so much as smearing it all over her woolen jacket. Her boots made a squishy sound as she turned around in a circle, trying to get her bearings. She could see nothing in the mist. But above her, she heard a vehicle stop. A few seconds later, a car door slammed. Looking up, she glimpsed a few stars between the skiffs of fog above her, but she had no clue whether she was facing the road or the ocean.

"Is anybody down there?" A male voice above and to her left called out.

Relief flooded through Wendy at the sound of a human voice. In fact, she reckoned she'd never heard such a wonderful voice. She turned in its direction and took a tentative step. Like a blind person feeling her way, she groped for something solid within reach. When her hands made contact with the slope of the hillside, she yelled back, "Yes, I'm here. To your left, I think . . . no, right." Now that she had his voice to aim for, she scrambled up the slope, using both hands and feet. "Keep talking," she said, puffing with exertion.

"Are you hurt?" He sounded closer, right above her.

"I'm okay," she answered, and, not realizing that she had reached the road, she continued clambering on all fours until her head butted something hard—his legs.

Arms reached down and lifted her with firm strength to a standing position. "You're safe now," he told her, holding her steady until she got her balance. She took a deep breath and then sneezed. She started shivering—the combination of wet clothes and reaction to her fall.

"Th-th-thank you," she stuttered, unable to stop shaking.

The man pulled her gently into the circle of his arms. His

body heat warmed her like a furnace. For a few seconds she rested there, waiting for her heart to slow down and her limbs to stop trembling. He murmured unintelligible words, as if comforting a scared child. For a few moments, Wendy felt safe, momentarily reminded of the security she had known long ago when her father would pick her up after a tumble—the security that had ended far too soon. She stopped shivering.

"Thanks again for your help," she murmured against his rough jacket. She pulled back, embarrassed to have given in to her weakness. Her rescuer's features were in shadows, as hers probably were to him. Good thing. With all the mud she had acquired on her person, she certainly could not look much like the professional nurse that she was.

Not that it mattered what he thought of her looks anyway. He was a man—a formidable one, judging by his height and breadth—but, nevertheless, a man. As far as Wendy was concerned, men were creatures to be cared for if they were sick and otherwise not to be counted on. The men in her life had not been great promise-keepers. Although Wendy's romantic soul had wanted to believe otherwise, she had been forced to conclude that her mother had been right: men were not worth the paper they wrote their fancy promises on.

With all that, Wendy found it troubling that it required effort to step away from the warm circle of this man's arms.

"I didn't even know if you were real," he said, his voice filled with relief. "One minute you were there, the next you were gone. I've been driving so long, I can hardly see straight, and this fog is a killer to drive in."

Wendy took another step back. Her limbs were already aching from either the fall or the climb; she wasn't sure which. In any case, she just wanted to get home. "Well, Mr. . . . uh, thanks for your help," she said, throwing back her shoulders and taking a step forward. "I'd better be going." Something told her that this man could be a threat to her peaceful, male-free life—the life she wanted. In these brief moments, he had managed to stir up feelings of need, feelings she had ruthlessly put down like a rabid animal, feelings that were warm and fuzzy at first but always ended in betrayal and heartache.

His vehicle was parked on the road, its headlights shining into the darkness. She started walking.

"Wait," he called. She stopped but didn't turn around. "You're going the wrong way." She heard the smile in his voice. "I turned the truck around to look for you."

Drat. She reversed direction. *Double drat.* "Thanks again."

"Can we give you a lift? You must be headed for the village."

We? He wasn't alone? Relief poured over her. Chivalrous man that he was, of course he would have a wife. Domesticated men were generally harmless, like defanged vipers. She relaxed, smiling at her own idiocy.

"Thank you very much. I would appreciate a lift to town," she said. "I'm afraid my fall down the rabbit hole has taken the fun out of the evening. And it seems I require a change of clothes, a bath, and a large scrub brush. By the way, is your truck insured for mud damage?"

He chuckled. "It's a farm truck. Don't worry about a little mud. I'm just relieved that you're okay."

While they had been talking, a stout figure got out of the vehicle and began approaching them. "Hey, boss, let's get going," a gravelly voice called out. "This damp ain't no good for a body."

Another man? Her curiosity meter rose.

"You're right, Horace. Shall we get going, ma'am?" he said, leading her to the pickup parked nearby. After opening the passenger door for her, he walked around to the driver's side and got in.

Horace was now beside her. "Hop in," he told her in that distinct Al Pacino voice that made Wendy think of gangsters. "We have to get to Shadow Ridge fast. Two days' driving nonstop— we need some sleep."

As she stood by the open passenger door, the light inside the truck gave Wendy her first look at her rescuer. He turned to watch them get in, and she saw the dark circles under his star-tling blue eyes, confirming his need of sleep. But he looked more than tired; he looked ill. His complexion, already pale, looked ghostly next to his dark stubble. Well, she couldn't afford to worry about him right now; she had to worry about herself.

If she were still in Vancouver, she never would have consid-ered getting into a truck with these characters. They could be crazed murderers; her rescuer had certainly been strong enough. On the other hand, Wendy had heard genuine exhaustion in his voice. She also remembered the comfort of those strong arms. Instinctively she knew that this man was not a killer. If he was the boss, as Horace called him, she figured she would be safe enough for a two-minute drive to town. Letting Horace slide in first, Wendy climbed in beside him and slammed the door shut.

Questions flooded her mind, but before she could phrase even one that didn't sound paranoid or rude, she saw the few lights of Shadow Ridge ahead. Brigadoon-like, the village material-ized out of the mist.

Her rescuer drove down the main street, slowing to a crawl. He glanced over at her. "Where do you live?"

They passed Meg's Café, the grocery store, the hardware store, and the bank. They were nearing the "cop shop" when she said, "Right here is fine, Mr. . . . ?"

He stopped immediately and peered out both sides of the truck. "Are you sure? The only thing here looks like the police station. And the name is Tremaine, Eric Tremaine."

He could have said, "Bond, James Bond" just as easily, Wendy thought, and she felt a bubble of laughter well up. She stifled it. "Our law enforcement here is the RCMP. They always get their man, you know." He nodded but didn't respond to the well-known reference to the Canadian Mounties. Perhaps he had been off the planet recently. She opened her door and jumped out. "This is just fine. Thanks for the ride, Mr. Tremaine."

"It's the least I could do after practically running you down back there. Now, can you direct me to the hotel?" Tremaine leaned over Horace to hear her directions. His cobalt eyes immobilized her.

The man himself, however, looked like death walking. She knew he would get little rest in the decrepit watering hole that passed for the town's only hotel. "I can, but if you want sleep, I would recommend the Raven Motel—one block back and turn left. It's newer, and you'll get quieter accommodations."

"Thanks, Miss . . . ? I never caught your name—" His question was swallowed up in the slamming door. She was gone.

The fog was less dense in town, and Wendy knew her way in the dark. She sprinted around the RCMP building, through the backyard, across the road, and up the hill past the hospital to the employees' residence, her home for the last year. Leaving her filthy boots on the porch, she stole in quietly, hoping to reach her room before anyone saw her. Unfortunately, just as she crossed the foyer and reached the bottom step that would take her to her second-floor bedroom, a young woman came out of the family room, saw Wendy, and stopped dead in her tracks.

"Good grief, Wendy, what happened to you?"

"Connie, what a surprise." There was no way to hide the fact that she had fallen in the mud. She gave her fellow nurse an abbreviated version of the mishap, omitting any mention of the two strangers who had driven her home. "I'm okay, really," Wendy added. "I just want a hot bath." She was too tired to face further questions. "A good soak will make everything right as rain." She paused on the second step. "It occurs to me that whoever coined that phrase never lived on the Pacific coast."

Rather than the smile Wendy hoped for, Connie's face settled into a frown. Wendy had a secret wish to see her much-too-serious co-worker laugh uncontrollably someday. Evidently, that wish would not be granted this evening.

"Joe Chandler called . . . several times. He seems eager to talk to you." Connie managed to sound exactly like a mother disapproving of a teenaged daughter's interest in boys. Exactly like Wendy's mother, as a matter of fact.

"Didn't you tell him I was having supper with Nani Williams in the village?"

"Is that where you were? I guess I forgot," Connie said before she toddled off to her room on the main floor.

"Whatever," murmured Wendy. She climbed the stairs and tiptoed down the hall to her own room. Turning on the light, she closed the door and sighed. When she caught a glimpse of herself in the mirror, she almost let out a yelp. She looked worse than she had suspected. Carefully, she peeled off her mud-caked coat and jeans. She rolled them up and shoved them into a corner, wondering if they were even salvageable. After putting on her robe and warm slippers, she walked to the communal bathroom.

While the tub filled with hot water, Wendy added a bubbly scent cube. Why not? She deserved it after her stressful evening. While she soothed her aches away in the tub, she kept her musings about the strangers at bay by turning her thoughts to Dr. Joe Chandler. He worried her. She could no longer deny that he had feelings for her. The problem was that she didn't—and couldn't—return them. Other than his gender, there was nothing wrong with him that she could put her finger on. Joe was a fine doctor, even if he didn't dress the part and tended to brood. Having no sense of humor certainly wasn't a crime. But even apart from her resolution to avoid romantic entanglement, she felt nothing for Joe, nothing whatsoever. And she knew she never would. It might be kinder to tell him sooner than later, she thought. But how? She had no idea.

The water cooled. Wendy left the tub and dried herself. Pulling her warmest flannel nightgown over her head, she debated returning Joe's call. Up to now, his attentions had been mildly flirtatious, but he had begun to press his suit more enthusiastically than she appreciated. He seemed singularly dense when it came to her indifference to him.

She decided to put off talking to Joe for the time being. Not returning his call might let him know where he stood. In any case, she'd be seeing him at work in a few hours. For now, he would just have to wait. She trundled off to bed and was asleep in minutes.

Eric Tremaine parked his truck outside the Raven Motel. He and Horace had to pound on the door for several minutes before the proprietor finally came to the desk and gave them a room. Horace brought in their two suitcases and set them down on the thin carpet.

Eric tossed his jacket across one of the beds. "I'd hate to think what the hotel is like if this is better," he commented as he surveyed the spartan accommodations. He stepped to the bathroom and flicked on the light. Turning the tap in the sink produced an agonized groaning in the pipes, followed by a spurt of icy brown water before a clear stream emerged. Grateful for the cold, Eric splashed his face several times. He felt more tired than he could remember.

"I suppose we can't expect much from a place that's not even on the map. How on earth did Scott get so far off the beaten path? And why Canada?"

All this thinking increased Eric's headache. His muscles felt as if sailors had tied knots in them. He closed his eyes against the light.

"You don't look so good, boss," Horace said, his face a mix of concern and fear. He tested the twin mattresses and pointed to the one near the window. "Here, take that one. Get some sleep."

"A few hours are all I need, Horace. Everything else can wait till morning." Eric stripped to his underwear, turned back the sheets, and slid between them. The cool linen felt like ice against his hot body, and he shivered for several minutes while his temperature rose. As he sank into a fitful doze, he muttered, "Horace, don't do anything without me tomorrow."

Throughout the long night, as he floated between sleep and delirium, vivid images of a ragamuffin with the most incredible eyes he had ever seen flitted around in his mind. Was she real, the mystery woman, or a product of his raging fever?

Chapter Two

Wendy held the medicine cup out to her patient in the wheelchair, then let out an exasperated sigh. "Phoebe dear, please swallow your heart pill. Surely you don't want it by injection again."

Phoebe Littlefeather clamped her lips shut and shook her head emphatically. Her small black eyes glistened with rebellion. Wendy recognized the signs of battle. She also noted her patient's leathery brown hands poised on the wheels of her wheelchair. Phoebe was about to make a break for it. It was a game the two had played more than once.

Someone called Wendy's name, and she turned around. Chuckling with childlike glee, Phoebe made her getaway down the corridor, pumping her wheels with remarkable strength, considering her age and heart condition.

"She did it again, Janet," Wendy said to the nurse who had been Phoebe's unwitting accomplice. "She still doesn't trust the white man's medicine."

Janet shrugged. "What can we do? No matter how many times she's come in here half dead and then walked out on her own two feet, she still has more faith in that chieftain's necklace around her neck than us. By the way, that is quite the bauble. Have you seen it?"

"Yes, and it is beautiful, but I'm afraid my faith is in God and Digoxin, not a necklace. It seems that we haven't made much progress after all." She started toward the med room. "I'm going to have to give this to her by injection again."

"Even if Phoebe has no faith in us, her family keeps bringing her here, so that's something," Janet said. Then she added, "Dr. Chandler sent over an OB patient from the clinic. She's in early labor but not doing much right now. I admitted her."

"Thanks. I'll look in on her after I give this to our girl." She exchanged the pills in the medicine cup for a vial and syringe. Janet lingered. "Anything else?"

"Yes. It's time for coffee. Phoebe's not going anywhere, and that lady's not going to have her baby in the next fifteen minutes. Come on."

Wendy smiled. "Has anyone ever told you that you're bossy?"

"Several ex-husbands and one or two boyfriends." She turned to go. "You know where to find me." Janet headed for the kitchen.

After giving her injection and checking in on her new patient, Wendy helped herself to a mug of steaming black coffee from the kitchen and took it through to the adjoining dining room. She was still barely a few steps away from the wards and would be able to hear a child cry, a patient's call bell, or anyone summoning her.

When she walked into the dining room, the hum of conversation stopped as everyone greeted her. She responded with a friendly wave. The place was unusually busy for a Saturday morning, she observed. Even Mrs. Welsh, the Director of Nursing, was there. Dr. Thomas, in deep conversation with Velma, the admitting clerk, ignored her, while Maxine, the housekeeper, was laughing at one of Janet's racy jokes.

Wendy's glance collided with Joe Chandler's accusing stare. It felt like a tangible thing. Her smile faded. She gave him a brief nod and found a chair at the opposite end of the long table.

"I'm surprised to see you here on a Saturday, Mrs. Welsh," Wendy said, addressing the gray-haired, portly woman sitting next to Janet. "Is there a problem?"

"I'm just checking my inventory and putting my supply order in today. Can you girls think of anything else we need besides antibiotics?" She included Janet in the question.

Wendy shook her head. "I believe we're okay now that the flu epidemic is pretty much over. Our last case is going home today."

"I'm just glad none of you nurses got sick," said Mrs. Welsh, "what with me working you so much this past month."

"Think nothing of it, boss," Janet remarked, taking a bite of a leftover biscuit. "Nurses never get sick. Or have to go to the bathroom. Those are well-known, documented facts."

Janet finished her last gulp of coffee and got up. Wendy followed suit, but Janet pushed her gently back into her chair. "It took you all of twenty minutes to get here; you have twenty left. Make good use of them."

Mrs. Welsh added, "Nurses need to recharge their batteries, Wendy. Take your full break."

Wendy sat down. She was not about to argue with her boss. Chairs scraped the floor as everyone seemed to get up at once, and she was left alone at the long table. The peacefulness of the sunny March morning washed over her, and she sipped her coffee. Her thoughts zeroed in on Eric Tremaine. Where was he now? More to the point, *how* was he? Down with the flu, probably. She might even run into him on the street at some point. It was highly likely in such a small town. Or had he left Shadow Ridge already? Somehow, she could not believe he would spend two days and nights driving here, only to leave twenty-four hours later. He had come for a reason, she was sure. Shadow Ridge was at the end of the highway; no one who drove here was just passing through.

Joe came through the swinging door from the kitchen just

then and interrupted Wendy's musings. He dropped down beside her, stethoscope dangling around his neck. "You didn't return my phone calls yesterday," he said. "Where were you all evening?"

His lord-of-the-manor attitude irritated her today. He made her feel as if she had missed her curfew. First Connie, now Joe; when had they become her parents? "I was out doing a home visit," she said, finishing the last swallow of coffee. She pushed her chair away from the table.

"You didn't return my call last night either." Again, that note of accusation.

"No, I didn't. I got in late and knew I'd see you today. Was it something important, something that couldn't wait a few hours?"

"Only to me, I guess." He pushed his chair back so hard, it tipped over. Not even bothering to pick it up, he stalked out.

Wendy exhaled slowly. All this because she didn't return a call? She had never seen Joe so angry. Obviously she had underestimated the strength of his feelings. Or was there something else bothering him? She knew that he was carrying a huge workload since Dr. Barton had taken a sudden extended leave last month. Was that enough to explain the outburst? She felt out of her depth but didn't know who to talk to about it. Carefully, she set Joe's chair back in place and left the dining room.

Wendy had little time that morning to worry about Joe Chandler. She spent much of it with Kay Duncan, her labor patient. This was Kay's first baby, and her husband was somewhere in the bush felling trees. A message had been sent, but there was no guarantee he would get here in time. Kay had no family nearby, so she needed a lot of reassurance. As soon as Wendy could, she returned to the desk to tackle the tedious paperwork that went along with the more satisfying hands-on nursing.

She was making some headway when she heard the booming voice of Dr. Thomas. Observing his brisk, no-nonsense approach, Wendy smiled. His unbuttoned lab coat rippled out around him, and with his spectacles and unruly iron gray hair, he looked more like an absentminded professor than the brilliant doctor that he was. The sheer vitality of the man was infectious.

"Ah, Wendy, my girl. I'm admitting a new patient, a young fella. Septicemia, from a nasty scratch that went untreated. No isolation precautions needed." He sat down beside her, took a blank chart out, and riffled through the pages until he pulled out a Doctor's Order sheet. Scribbling furiously, he talked at the same time. "We'll give him our strongest IV antibiotics for a couple of days, and he'll be on his feet in no time. He looks healthy enough otherwise, but with a temperature of a hundred and four he's down for the count today. Got a bed for him?"

Wendy checked her Kardex and assigned him the room nearest the desk. "I think we'd better have him close by," she said, as she tried to pull the scattered chart pages together.

Dr. Thomas kept writing. "This young man's not from around here, apparently. He's staying at the motel. A friend brought him here late this morning in pretty bad shape." He finished writing his orders, and Wendy looked at the familiar scrawl. Either his writing was improving, or she was getting used to it. "Name's Eric Tremaine."

Although she knew it had to be *that man*—she had seen how sick he looked less than twenty-four hours ago—her heart jumped at hearing the name. She was helpless to control the telltale color that crept into her face. Aiming for a casual, professional interest, she said, "A stranger, you say. I wonder what he's doing this far from civilization."

"Good question." He stopped writing and flipped to the information sheet on the chart. "I see that he's from the Seattle area, with occupation listed as rancher. That would explain how a cut could go septic so quickly."

Wendy raised her eyebrows. Her friend, Scott Ellerslie, had come from a ranching town near Seattle. It could be coincidence, she thought. Or not.

Dr. Thomas peered at her over his spectacles. "Are you feeling all right, Wendy? You're looking a little flushed." He put a cool hand to her forehead. "No fever. Can't have my favorite nurse getting sick, can I?" He stood up. "Well, I've got to get to the clinic. I'm on today—again. Chandler and I have been running on fumes this past month, what with Dr. Barton away and this nasty flu epidemic. Uh, speaking of Joe, I just ran into him, and he looked like the very devil."

Wendy said nothing, but she could tell that Dr. Thomas had something on his mind. He was fiddling with papers and looking anywhere but at her. He cleared his throat. "Lack of sleep and a frustrated love life will do that to a man." He looked at his watch and straightened a pile of requisitions. "Is there anything you want to tell me?" He slid a quick glance at her.

Wendy wanted nothing more than to pour out her fears and concerns about Joe to someone, but she hesitated. She hated to gossip. On the other hand, she needed some wisdom right now, and if she trusted any man, she trusted Dr. Thomas. "You aren't as nearsighted as you'd have us all believe, Dr. Thomas," she said with a wry smile. "I don't know what to do about Joe. He was angry with me today, and I confess, it scared me a little."

The doctor took off his glasses and examined the lenses for smudges. He took a handkerchief out of his pocket and wiped them. "Wendy, I make it a policy not to interfere in matters of the heart, but when it starts affecting work, I have to say something." He looked through his glasses and then wiped them some more. "My advice to you is simple: let Joe know how you feel about him—or, rather, how you don't feel—and soon. He needs to stop hoping in a lost cause." Dr. Thomas replaced his spectacles, apparently satisfied. "He'll be upset, but he'll get over it. With our being so stretched, I need him focused on work."

"What makes you think I don't return Joe's feelings?"

"My dear, I'm a keen observer of body language. Let's just say you have a 'no trespassing' sign written all over you."

"You mean I'm unfriendly?"

"No, of course not. You are warmth and caring itself to patients and your friends. But men approach at their own risk. I think Joe hoped he would be the exception. At any rate, I hate to interfere with anyone's personal life, but it might help to let Chandler know straight up that he hasn't got a prayer." He gave her a paternal pat on the shoulder and winked. "As for this new one"—he stood up and pointed to Eric's chart— "antibiotics and your usual TLC will get him on his feet in no time." He threw the words over his shoulder on his way out.

Wendy sat for a moment after Dr. Thomas had gone. She was relieved that he had spoken to her, that he was aware of Joe's anger and unwanted attentions. Although it was a joke among the nurses that Wendy was a man-hater, it was not strictly true. Just because she had sworn off them, like cigarettes, didn't mean she hated them. That emotion was too strong. She simply had no interest in having a relationship with one. She had hoped that Joe would see that, but after that display of temper in the dining room, she realized Dr. Thomas was right—she needed to be crystal clear about things. The sooner, the better.

That decided, she skimmed through Eric's chart and checked Dr. Thomas' orders. She noted that Eric's marital status was listed as single. Which didn't mean anything, really, these days. Closing the chart, she stood up and headed to see her new patient. As she walked, her professional mantle settled on her. Wendy knew she was gifted with a calm, reassuring manner. For the most part, it matched her inner core of steadiness, but right now her heart was quickening at the thought of seeing her rescuer once again, this time on her own turf.

When she walked into the emergency room, Eric Tremaine was lying on the stretcher, covered by a flannel sheet. His complexion, no longer pasty, was now flushed. Heavy stubble darkened his jaw, making him appear dangerous, even in his fever-induced stupor.

"He's burning up, Wendy. I just left him in his briefs to let his skin breathe," Janet told her, getting the room ready for the next patient. "And I put a dressing on his wound."

"That's fine," Wendy murmured. "Is Horace still here?" she asked.

"Who?"

"His friend. The one who brought him in today?"

"Oh, you mean the gangsterlike character? Beats me." She shrugged. "Say, how did you know his name? He wouldn't give it to me, like it was a state secret."

Wendy shrugged. "We all sort of . . . ran into each other last night."

Janet's eyes widened with surprise. "Wendy Hunt, you have to be the most closemouthed person I know," Janet said, laughing. "Well, Miss Full-of-Secrets, come on, give. What's the deal? How did you meet him?"

Just then Eric opened his eyes, fixed them firmly on Wendy, and called out, "Scott, please listen to me!" His eyes closed.

Wendy's eyes widened. "Could he mean Scott Ellerslie?"

Janet looked skeptical. "Scott's a pretty common name, don't you think? It's probably just coincidence."

"Except that they both live in the Seattle area. What if Eric Tremaine and his friend know Scott and came here to see him?"

"If they did, they've come a long way for nothing—which they'll find out soon enough. How long has it been since he left? A month?"

"Three weeks tomorrow," Wendy said. She regretted the words as soon as she said them.

Janet raised her eyebrows. "Not that you're counting or anything."

Wendy sighed. "Give it a rest, will you, please? How many times do I have to repeat it? We were friends, nothing more. Subject closed." She started pushing the gurney out of the room. "Let's just get our patient to a bed. I want him next to the front desk. He's the sickest one here right now."

They pushed the stretcher down the hall in silence for a few seconds, but Janet was like a dog with a bone. "I'd guess that meeting last night with Eric Tremaine was on the earth-shaking scale. I do believe you're staring at his bare chest, your mouth is open, and you're drooling." She tapped the side of her mouth to emphasize her point.

"And I believe you must be looking in the mirror," Wendy said. "Just because you can't stand being without a man doesn't mean I need one. The fact is, I'm done with them, no matter how attractive they may be."

"Well, at least you admit he's attractive. You must still have a pulse. Men can be pleasant diversions, as long as you don't take them too seriously."

They steered the stretcher into Eric's room and brought it even with the bed. With practiced efficiency, they quickly transferred him from gurney to bed. After they moved him, Wendy checked his dressing for oozing, but so far it remained dry and intact. Janet continued their conversation while she automatically straightened his bedclothes. "You may have yourself convinced, but I'm not buying that load of sheep dip— pardon my French. I refuse to believe that you would rather feel half alive for the rest of your short, lonely life than experience the heights of passionate love."

"Look, it's a trust issue, okay? The men in my life have been less than faithful, and I'd prefer not to rush into another relationship, especially with—"

"Someone who can't give you an ironclad guarantee to never leave you?" Janet finished the thought for her.

"A man, exactly." Wendy nodded. "And FYI, no one ever died of abstinence."

Janet shuddered. "That is something I never want to catch, thank you very much."

Eric moved restlessly on the bed, muttering softly. Janet watched him for a minute, then told him, "You've got the perfect challenge, Mr. Tremaine, if you like the hard-to-get type."

Wendy checked his IV and pulled up his bed rail. "Very amusing, Janet."

Eric stirred again, this time opening his eyes. His vacant stare, so unsettling, zeroed in on Wendy again, and he said breathlessly, "Don't tell anyone about this. . . ." His eyes closed, and he fell into a deeper slumber.

"Well, well. A man with secrets—my favorite kind," Janet quipped.

"They're all your favorite kind, Miss J. But think about this for a minute, if you can. This man may not be as harmless as he appears right now. I would think you'd be more cautious about encouraging him to pursue one of your friends." She left the room and hoped Janet would rethink her matchmaking efforts.

As it was, Wendy was trying hard to forget the feelings Eric Tremaine had stirred up and the sense of belonging she'd felt in his arms. Could she keep him out of her mind and heart until he left? Surely whatever had brought him to Shadow Ridge would not keep him here for long.

A man was waiting at the desk when Wendy returned. She stopped short at the sight of him peering over the counter at the charts. Outfitted in black, he wore a leather jacket over a dark T-shirt, with black jeans and sneakers. His head was concealed by a black toque, which he snatched off when he saw Wendy. The thick mat of pure white hair contrasted sharply with the rest of him. From the way he was wringing the life out of that poor toque, it was obvious he was upset.

"Can I help you?"

"I hope so, ma'am. I'm looking for Eric Tremaine. I brought him in a while ago."

As soon as he spoke, she realized it was Horace. The gravelly voice was unmistakable. Obviously, he didn't recognize her either. Why would he? She had looked like a mangled cat the last time they'd met.

Wendy studied his weather-beaten face, lined with at least six decades of living. Horace turned, and she saw the scar—a long, jagged line extending down the right side of his face. She had not been far off comparing him to Al Pacino. Hadn't he played in *Scarface*? She could be face-to-face with a real-live gangster. And if Horace was a gangster, would that make Eric Tremaine the godfather? She had to smile. In the light of day, the idea seemed too absurd to take seriously. She decided to reserve judgment on the gangster theory until she had more facts.

"Mr. Tremaine has been admitted. Your name is . . . ?"

"Ma'am, I need to see him."

Wendy was not going to get much out of him if he wouldn't even give her his name.

"He's in no condition to see any visitors right now. In fact, he's sleeping." Horace's knitted cap was taking quite a beating. Wendy tried again. "So, what brings you two here, all the way from . . . Seattle, was it?"

Horace stopped fidgeting with the toque. He stared at Wendy, who suddenly felt pinned under a microscope. After she had begun to think he was not going to answer at all, he said, "Business." He must have decided that small bit of information was need-to-know. "When will he be awake?"

Her detective skills might be lacking, but Wendy's nosiness made up for it. "He's not really awake, but I'll let you peek in—just for a minute." She led him to Eric's room and watched relief flood Horace's face at the sight of his boss. She hovered outside the door, hoping to learn something, but Horace stayed only long enough to make sure that Eric was sleeping and then left. She would bet the farm that Horace would return again soon.

Her labor patient, who had progressed considerably, summoned Wendy. She was relieved that Kay's husband, dripping sawdust everywhere, had arrived; within the hour he was presented with an eight-pound, seven-ounce girl.

Wendy's eyes filled when she saw Kay's husband tenderly kiss his wife. Could such a loving man one day find cause to leave his daughter, as Wendy's father had? Would Charlie Duncan one day walk away from his family, move on to greener pastures, betray his wife and desert his daughter? *Dear God, no,* Wendy silently prayed. Of all people, Wendy knew the price they would pay.

Wendy made a final check on the wards. Eric remained in a

restless stupor, his fever still high despite the medications he was receiving. When she looked in on him, Janet was taking his blood pressure. He was still restless, and his eyes opened from time to time, but he remained unaware of his surroundings.

"Temp's still a hundred and three, Wendy. I just gave him another acetaminophen suppository. He's been delirious, talking a lot, but nothing that makes any sense."

Wendy hung his IV antibiotic and left the room. It was time to hand over the responsibility to the next shift and give her reports. Connie and Sarah had arrived to take charge.

After reporting was over, Connie said, "Would you mind switching shifts with me tomorrow, Wendy?" she asked. "I'll work your day, if you can work my evening."

"No problem," Wendy replied. "I have no plans."

"Did you ever call Joe, by the way?"

Wendy felt the censure behind the casual inquiry. "Not last night, but I saw him this morning." She had an urge to tell Connie that it was not her job to make sure that Wendy returned calls, that she was not Wendy's keeper. It was almost as if Connie felt she had to protect Joe's interests.

Just then, Horace rushed through the front door. He made a beeline for Wendy. "Oh, there you are, ma'am. I gotta see Mr. Tremaine right now. Is he awake yet?" The urgency was palpable. Horace seemed even more agitated than earlier.

"He wasn't a few minutes ago—"

"I gotta see him. It's important, ma'am. Truly."

Gangster business? She repressed a smile. "Well, all right, you can see him, if he's awake." She started toward Eric's room. "I'll check."

Wendy approached Eric's bed quietly. She heard his even breathing—a good sign that he had passed from delirium into a peaceful sleep. She stood beside the bed for a few moments. Without warning, his eyes opened, and he grabbed Wendy's arm in a viselike grip. Electricity shot through her. With her free hand, she tried to pull her arm free, but he squeezed harder.

Although his cheeks were still flushed, his eyes were clear. "Are you real?" he asked.

His question didn't make sense. Wendy touched his forehead briefly. His temperature was still about a hundred but not much more than that, she guessed. He couldn't be delirious; he must be confused.

"It's all right, Eric," she said in her calm, soothing voice. "I'm a nurse, and you're in the hospital. How are you feeling?"

Eric turned the full force of his gaze on her. The clear blue eyes that had haunted Wendy now looked her over carefully from head to toe. How had she thought he was confused? Eric lingered over her curves, and when he finally met her eyes, she felt he knew her as well as her doctor did.

She tugged sharply, and he released her arm, which caused her to stumble backward a bit. His arm snaked around her waist to steady her. "Have we met before?"

Did she want to remind him of their first meeting? Probably not. "Surely you can do better than that old line, Mr. Tremaine." She forced herself to smile. Then she stepped out of his reach. His touch threatened her resolve to remain aloof.

Half sitting, he tried to position his two pillows behind him. The sheet fell to his waist, revealing his well-muscled chest. Wendy looked away.

"I do remember you," he murmured, closing his eyes. "At least, I think I do. . . . It's the eyes. . . ." She thought he was falling asleep again and moved to leave, but his voice stopped her—that wonderful, deep voice that had guided her from her pit of darkness, the voice she had been unable to erase since she had heard it. Eric opened his eyes, fastened them on her, and said, "I almost ran over you in the fog. That was you, wasn't it? I wasn't dreaming?"

He read her name tag. "W. Hunt, RN. What does the *W* stand for? Winnie? Wanda? Wynnona?"

His sheer masculinity beckoned her closer. Deliberately, she took another step back. In what she hoped was her most unapproachable professional manner, she told him that Horace was waiting to see him.

Horace, who had been standing at the door, came forward at Wendy's signal. He grabbed Eric's hand and pumped it up and down enthusiastically. Wendy suspected that Horace felt like hugging his boss but probably was self-conscious about such demonstrations of affection. There was no doubt that he was glad to see Eric, and from the genuine affection on Eric's face, it was mutual.

Eric looked much younger when he smiled so openly, as he did at Horace. "How are you doing, old friend?" He pulled his hand gently from Horace's tight grasp. "What have you been up to, while I've been sleeping the day away?" Wendy could see what Horace evidently did not: that Eric's spurt of energy was depleted. He needed more rest.

"I found out something. . . ." Horace began, and then he glanced meaningfully at Wendy. It was that wretched need-to-know basis again. She would learn nothing if she remained, so she stepped just outside the room, shamelessly eavesdropping. Connie's disapproving look convicted her of her atrocious behavior and drove her away from the door. Disgusted with herself, Wendy assuaged her guilt by answering a call bell, even though she was officially off duty.

Passing by Eric's room after attending to Phoebe, she heard Horace's distinctive voice saying, "Get some rest, boss. Don't worry 'bout nothin'."

Eric's response was softer but still audible. "Don't do anything until I get out of here. Remember the letter, Horace. Be careful."

Interesting. Wendy's vivid imagination was firing on all cylinders. She decided that she needed to know what was going on. She would march right in there and ask Eric straight out why he had come to British Columbia. Unfortunately, by the time she reached Eric's bedside, he had drifted off to sleep and was snoring softly.

Chapter Three

Having traded shifts with Connie the day before, Wendy slept in. She showered, dressed, and then went to the kitchen to make her breakfast. Although the staff was free to eat all their meals at the hospital—the job included room and board— everyone liked some time away from the workplace. As it was, the view from the small kitchen's windows overlooked the back of the hospital, so they were never very far away.

All the residents bought whatever food they wanted, to share or not, as each one chose. Anything that was not common property was labeled with the name of its owner. Staples, such as salt and pepper, bread, butter, tea, and coffee, were purchased as needed from a dorm fund.

Wendy went to the kitchen and fixed some scrambled eggs and toast and sat down. Out of respect for Shirley and Roxie, who had crawled into their beds that morning after night shifts, she tried to make as little noise as possible. The only other nurse at home was Jean, and Wendy had passed her in the hall a few minutes ago.

Although the dorm housed more than a dozen women, it never seemed crowded. The large upstairs living room held three sofas and two recliners facing a big-screen TV. Bookshelves jostled for wall space with a stereo system, and a fireplace added a cozy feel to the room. The picture window allowed a panoramic view of the town and the bay, with glass doors that opened onto a balcony.

Directly below the living room was another large common room. This one had been designed for group activities like Ping-Pong, board games, and for entertaining friends. A piano sat at one end of the room. A similar picture window looked out on the same ocean view as upstairs. The main difference in the common rooms was that male guests were permitted downstairs but not up; that rule was ironclad. If the women upstairs felt an urge to parade around in their undies, they could do so without fear of unexpected male intrusion.

Wendy was finishing her scrambled eggs when Jean wandered in, looking half asleep. She pulled her robe together and tied the belt. "G'morning," she said through a yawn. "I thought you were working today." It was more of an observation than a question. "Anything good around here?"

"There are a couple of eggs left and lots of bread and jam."

"I don't suppose we have any bacon," Jean said, opening the refrigerator and glancing in. "Nope. I guess it's cereal again." She helped herself to a bowl of oat flakes and sat down across from Wendy. The table had been positioned right in front of the window for the view. Looking out, she remarked, "It actually doesn't look too bad out there today. I can't tell you how sick I am of this weather. I have got to get back to civilization."

"Only three more weeks, and you will, Jean." Wendy sipped her coffee and looked out over the bay. Unlike Jean, Wendy had no desire to go back to city life. Not with what she had left behind there. Moreover, she never tired of this view. Every day it was different. Sometimes the ocean was green and cold. Other times, wind whipped up tiny whitecaps on the waves.

Today, the ocean was deep blue. Sunlight sparkled on the waves as if God had sprinkled diamonds on the sea.

"I love it here," she said. "It's peaceful. The pace is so slow and easy, I'm afraid I don't miss the big city at all."

Jean scowled. "You are such a positive person. Don't you ever get tired of being so up?" Jean was not a morning person; Wendy knew that and didn't waste time taking offense. It helped that she also knew that Jean was one of the best nurses they had. There would be a huge gap when she left.

"It looks so nice out, I thought I'd go beachcombing. I'd like to find some glass balls, the big ones. Do you want to come?"

Jean yawned. She scratched her head. "You're perky too. Don't you ever just sit around and do nothing?" She finished her cereal, got up, and put the bowl into the sink. "I'm going to curl up on the couch and read a book. Or watch the soaps. Knock yourself out looking for glass balls." Jean ambled out of the kitchen.

Wendy pushed away from the table, cleaned up the few dishes, and went to get ready for some serious beachcombing.

At 3:15 that afternoon, Wendy walked into the hospital, ready for work. She had almost forgotten Eric Tremaine and the feelings he stirred. Almost. After getting the day report from Connie, Wendy checked her patients' needs for the evening.

Eric was still on his IV antibiotics. Good. She would only have to hang up a dose and be done with it. Piece of cake. Then she noticed that he needed a dressing change. That would entail another few minutes in his presence, but she was a nurse, for goodness' sake—she could maintain her professional demeanor that long, surely. As long as she didn't have to see him more than that, she'd be fine.

She marched, head high, out of the medicine room—and right into Eric Tremaine's chest. Although there was no possible way he could know what Wendy had been cogitating about, hot color flooded her face. She backed up and lowered her head.

"Nice to run into you again, W. Hunt," he said, smiling and

emphasizing her initial. "You look a little flushed," he observed. "I hope you're not coming down with something."

I'm a professional, she reminded herself silently. *This is one of my patients.* She forced her eyes to meet his. "I'm just fine," she began, but she stopped when her eyes took in his changed appearance. Not only had the stubble disappeared, but the dark circles under his eyes and his unnatural color were gone as well. He didn't even have to push around an IV pole. Connie had locked off his IV site between antibiotic doses. He was the picture of health, of masculine vitality; he was simply stunning. Her heart lurched.

She grabbed the Kardex from the desk—she needed something solid to hold on to. "I'm very busy, so you'll have to excuse me." She had no goal other than to remove herself from the vicinity of Eric Tremaine. She walked away but felt his eyes boring into her back until she turned in at the utility room. She took a moment there to calm her jangling nerves. She was distressed by her lack of self-control where Eric Tremaine was concerned. Did he not see the no-trespassing sign Dr. Thomas had assured her was still in place? Did she have to draw him a diagram?

While she was at it, she would draw two, one for Joe Chandler as well. Remembering Scott Ellerslie, Wendy recalled how easy he was on her emotions, demanding nothing but friendship, offering nothing but warm and fuzzy feelings with no hint of physical attraction. In other words, they were just friends who enjoyed being together without the emotional minefield of sex or chemistry muddying the waters.

Wendy deliberately put Eric on a back burner of her mind so she could concentrate on her responsibilities for the evening ahead. Reminding herself once more that he was one of those untrustworthy creatures, a man, she took a deep breath and left the utility room to make her rounds.

Thirty minutes later, Wendy took Phoebe's blood-pressure medication to her room. The room was empty, forcing Wendy to search for her. After checking the patient lounge, she spotted Phoebe in her wheelchair, laughing delightedly. Eric Tremaine was kneeling beside the chair, talking to her. When he glanced up and saw Wendy, he smiled. Her intense and positive reaction to that smile made her understand how he had Phoebe Littlefeather giggling like a teenager. More than anything she wished she could turn and walk away, but Phoebe needed her medicine. Wendy had no choice but to move toward them.

"Do you have something for Phoebe, Ms. Hunt?" Eric asked as he wheeled the elderly native woman to meet Wendy halfway.

Phoebe giggled. "You're supposed to call her Wendy," she told Eric.

He grinned triumphantly. "Aha, the secret's out."

Miraculously, Phoebe took her medicine without argument or flight. *Eric Tremaine's persuasive powers at work?* "Supper will be coming soon, Phoebe," Wendy said. "You'd better get back to your room."

Eric gave her a mock bow. "You heard the boss lady, Phoebe. Allow me to drive." Eric wheeled Phoebe Littlefeather, giggling, to her room.

As soon as the supper trays arrived, Wendy and her nursing assistant, Helen, distributed them. Helen went to get her own meal, but by the time Wendy went for supper, the kitchen was cold, the dining room deserted. She grabbed a plate of food from the fridge, warmed it in the microwave, poured herself a cup of coffee, and plopped down at the end of the table. She propped her feet on the chair beside her, leaned back, and closed her eyes.

"Mind if I join you?" Eric Tremaine asked from the doorway.

Her eyes flew open, and she pulled her feet off the chair. "What are you doing here?" she demanded, as if Eric had walked into an operating room without a mask.

"Helen said it would be all right for me to come in." Wendy made a mental note to discuss boundaries with her colleague later. "I saw you head in here," he went on. "I thought you looked lonely."

"I'm not lonely," she said quickly. "But I do like to be alone at times." She waited, but he didn't take the hint. "Do you need something?"

"Just to talk, if that's okay. Am I contagious or something?"

You're something, all right, she thought, as butterflies danced around in her stomach. But apart from all that, he was also a patient, and one who needed to talk. She relented. "No, Mr. Tremaine, you're not contagious. Sit, if you like. Do you want some juice or coffee?"

"No thanks." He sat facing her, on the chair her shoes had just vacated.

She said nothing. Her food might as well have been sawdust, her mouth was so dry. Lifting the coffee cup to her lips, she started to sip just as he spoke. "Do you dislike me for some reason?" he asked.

She sputtered, and the coffee dribbled down her chin. She grabbed a napkin to wipe her mouth and said, "I beg your pardon?" He was constantly throwing her off balance.

He leaned forward, and she caught a whiff of his clean, male smell, a fragrance that must have been designed to attract every living, breathing female. "I've heard nothing but glowing reports about you from everyone. Even crotchety Mr. Peters thinks the sun rises and sets in you. Yet, you avoid me."

Wendy took a moment to think about his question. What was the best way to answer that? Be truthful? Tell him that he stirred up romantic urges she had buried after Richard betrayed her? No point in giving him that kind of advantage. She decided she had been diplomatic long enough. "I tend to be reserved with strangers, especially charming ones who ask too many questions." Her tone was a hairsbreadth away from condescending.

"So you think I'm charming?"

She gazed heavenward. Only a man could have interpreted her answer as a compliment. "It's a relative term. I meant it more like *oily*." Wendy pushed her plate of uneaten supper away. "You may think you know all about me, Mr. Tremaine, but I know nothing about you. Who are you? Where do you come from? Why are you here? And who is . . ." She almost said *Scott* but changed it to *Horace* instead.

He seemed completely unfazed by her intimidating tactics. "Ms. Hunt, I am an open book to you." He gave her another big smile, but she had hardened her heart against his charm. He would have to do more than smile sweetly to earn her trust. She waited.

"First of all, my name is Eric, not Mr. Tremaine. I live in a small town called Rosewood, near Seattle. I own a horse ranch, and Horace is my foreman."

Rosewood! Scott Ellerslie had come from Rosewood. This had to be more than coincidence, but what was the connection?

Before she could find out, Helen appeared in the doorway.

"Sorry to disturb your supper, but a couple of rowdies just showed up in Emergency. They've been in a knife fight. I called Dr. Thomas, but he's going to need you."

"Can I help?" Eric asked, following her out. She felt his hand touch her back. She stiffened. When he dropped his hand, the sensation of it lingered. She needed to counter his physical effect on her. "Not unless you're good with a needle and catgut," she said, with definite coolness. Eric Tremaine would not stay long in Shadow Ridge, and although her body was betraying her by responding to his touch, her heart was still whole. Once he left the hospital, she need never see him again.

It took over an hour to sew up the two brawlers. Both were drunk, both uncooperative. Dr. Thomas called the RCMP, and their only two constables were dispatched to the hospital. As soon as the cuts were sutured, the patients were handcuffed and taken away in the RCMP patrol car.

The time had come to give Eric his antibiotic and change his dressing. She pulled his medication out of the refrigerator and then picked up some alcohol swabs and a large syringe filled with saline. Eric's IV tubing had to be flushed before she could reconnect him to his drip. On the way to his room, she stopped at the clean utility room to get her sterile supplies.

Helen came in silently behind her. "Do you need any help?" she asked innocently.

Wendy nearly dropped everything. "Goodness, Helen! You startled me. Is there a problem with a patient?"

"No, dear. In fact, I can't believe how much better Mr. Tremaine is doing. I walked by the TV room, and he had old Mr. Peters laughing and chattering like a magpie. And you know how grouchy he can be—Mr. Peters, I mean, not Mr. Tremaine. I just think he's awfully charming. Mr. Tremaine, I mean. He makes me feel like a young girl again." She giggled.

Wendy sighed. Helen had officially fallen under Eric's spell. Phoebe Littlefeather, Mr. Peters, now Helen. Was anyone immune? "I concede that anyone who can make Mr. Peters laugh is quite something," Wendy said. Helen didn't seem to notice anything amiss and trotted off down the hall to finish getting patients ready for bed.

Wendy took her meds, the dressing materials, and her professional dignity to Eric's room. He was propped up in bed reading a letter, which he slipped under the sheets as soon as he saw her. He looked guilty, she thought, which intrigued her. What was in the letter? Was this the one he had mentioned to Horace? That letter might explain a lot. For a few seconds, Wendy considered ways to extract it from under the sheets, but Eric interrupted her thoughts.

"Have you come to interrogate me, ma'am?" he asked, with an engaging, lopsided smile. "What's that in your hand? Truth serum?"

She could not stop a smile from spreading across her face. He had no idea how much she wished she did hold a potion that would make him spill his guts instead of the harmless saline solution. She did her best to adopt a professional expression. Holding up the syringe so he could get a good look at, she flicked the air bubble out and said, "This is so I can hook you back up to your IV, Mr. Tremaine. Ready?"

He rolled up his left pajama sleeve.

Bending over his arm, Wendy felt his eyes watching her every move. Cheeks burning, she wasted no time flushing the site and hooking him back up to his IV bag. After hanging the medication, she said briskly, "Now, would you please roll over so I can change your dressing?"

He unbuttoned his shirt, flipped over onto his stomach, and said, "Have at it. It hardly hurts anymore, thanks to your excellent care."

"That's a relief," she said with a smile. "We do try to leave you better than we found you." She lifted his shirt up and was pleased to see no oozing on the gauze. She removed the tape carefully and discarded the dressing. He didn't flinch. "I'm happy to say that your infection looks much better. The redness around the wound is almost gone." She put a fresh four-by-four gauze pad on it and a piece of elastic bandage to keep it in place.

"You have a very gentle touch. It feels a lot better, thank you," Eric said, turning around. He sat up to button his shirt, then swung his legs over the side of the bed.

"You're welcome." Glad the event was over, she sighed with relief. By her calculations, she shouldn't have to spend any more time with him this evening, other than to check him at the end of the shift. With any luck, after that, they would never cross paths again. She turned to leave, but in her haste to escape Eric's room, she tripped over the wastebasket. From the corner of her eye she saw his arms reach out, and, before she hit the floor, he grabbed her from behind and pulled her back against his chest. She went limp, grateful to be upright.

It took a few seconds for her to realize that his arms had tightened around her. Then she felt his lips against her hair. Her heart pounded in her chest as his breath brushed her cheeks. Unable to pull away, she leaned against him, experiencing a sense of belonging she had never felt before. Through her uniform she felt his warmth and heard his breathing quicken. Turning her in his arms, he pulled her close. Somewhere in her mind, a neon sign flashed *danger ahead,* but her limbs refused to heed it. She felt safer than she could ever remember; she had to stay.

For several moments she remained securely held in Eric's arms as the world faded away. Nothing else was real. At length, Eric gently set her away from him, and his gaze traveled over her face to settle on her lips. *He's going to kiss me,* Wendy thought just before his face descended. She made no effort to resist him. She couldn't.

"Wendy," he whispered close to her lips. "You are such a tempting little thing. But I can't let myself be distracted from my purpose, especially by you." Abruptly, he planted a firm, fatherly kiss on her forehead and released her. He leaned back from her, his face unreadable.

Outside the circle of his arms, cold reality hit Wendy forcefully. She had played right into his hands, no better than Phoebe, Helen, or Mr. Peters. How could she have let this happen? He was good; she'd give him that. But she was Wendy Hunt, the man-hater, and she couldn't let him get away with this. Her eyes filled, but she held the tears back by sheer will. Although she felt used and thrown away, he would never know it. What was it he had said, that she was a tempting little thing but a distraction from some grand purpose? Hah!

"I must attend to some life-and-death matters as well, Mr. Tremaine," she said as coldly as she could in a voice that wouldn't rise above a whisper. "Excuse me." Turning on her heel, she walked out. For the last time, she hoped.

Wendy went through the motions of working, but her heart felt like a stone. She kept replaying the scene in Eric's room and puzzling over his words. What important purpose could he have that she was distracting him from? It didn't salvage her bruised ego, but it did provide something else to focus on besides her physical vulnerability to him.

She felt a light tap on her shoulder two hours later. "Excuse me, Wendy." It was Helen.

"Yes?"

The older woman looked worried. "That nice Eric Tremaine is needing something for a headache."

Good, Wendy thought, her own heart aching. Aloud, she asked, "Did he request a painkiller?"

"Not exactly, dear. When I went in to check his dressing, he mentioned that he had a splitting headache. It looks like he really needs something, or I don't think he'll sleep tonight. He probably overdid things today, feeling so much better, and all."

"I see. Well, thanks." Helen kept standing there. "Is there something else?"

"You know, Wendy, I think he likes you. He's asked me a lot of questions about you."

Wendy said nothing. A call bell rang. As if on cue, it was Eric, asking for an analgesic. Sighing, Wendy went to check his orders. He had questions about her, did he? Well, she had plenty of her own. The first one was, how could she face him after the recent debacle in his room? She had been regretting her totally unprofessional behavior since she left. Moreover, she was ashamed that she had given in to the feelings he aroused in her.

She weighed her options. There were none. Helen was not qualified to give medications. Wendy put two white pills into a medicine cup, decided to act as if nothing had happened, and went to his room.

As soon as Eric saw Wendy enter his room, he pulled himself to a sitting position and tucked his pillow behind him. He watched her cross to his bed, pour a glass of water, and hand him the pills. When she finally glanced at him, her expression was unreadable.

He resisted the strong urge to take her into his arms and kiss away her hurt. He had been berating himself for two hours. He never should have allowed his desire to overcome his good sense. She had felt so soft, so yielding in his arms, that he had let his passion get the better of him. Thankfully, he had been able to regain some self-control before he kissed her. He could not lose focus on his goal, and she threatened that focus. It was ironic that only tonight, after talking to Helen, had he discovered that Wendy might be the key to his success.

He needed her cooperation, but how to get it after what had transpired between them? Her reaction told him he had hurt her. Moreover, he could see in the eyes she turned on him that she was not about to engage in unnecessary conversation.

She had given him the pills without a word. "Thank you," he said, downing them with a gulp of water. "I've been doing a lot of thinking today."

"No wonder you have a headache."

Wonderful! She still had a spark of fight left. "Still a prickly little hedgehog, I see." She turned to go, and he reached out. He would have grabbed her arm, but she saw it coming and twisted out of reach. "Wait, Wendy. Please don't go. I want to apologize . . . for earlier." *Blast,* she was so far away from him. How could he bridge this huge gap that his own actions had created?

"Least said, soonest mended, Mr. Tremaine. Nothing happened . . . earlier."

"I need your help," he said, desperate to keep her from leaving before he could break through to her. "I came here to find Scott Ellerslie. I understand you two were good friends." He had heard it was more than friends, but he didn't want to say that.

She stopped backing away. "What is your business with Scott?"

What a protective tiger she was about his younger brother. Eric experienced a pang of sibling jealousy. Scott was definitely high on Wendy's list of friends. He watched her expression as he revealed the answer. "Scott Ellerslie is my brother."

He saw several emotions come and go on her transparent

face. At length, after taking a deep breath, she finally said, "So, you're the tyrannical older brother Scott mentioned? Your names are different."

Tyrannical? Scott had evidently laid it on thick, although Eric couldn't have expected his brother to be complimentary, not after their parting. "Our fathers were different. Same mother. Obviously, Scott mentioned me."

"Once or twice."

"We didn't part on the best of terms," he said, the understatement lost on Wendy. Eric could still remember the sound of the ranch house door slamming behind Scott's angry exit.

"It wasn't so much what he said about you but what he said about himself that told me what kind of person you were. Nothing he did ever measured up to your standards. Whenever he was proud of an accomplishment, you found some tiny flaw in it that diminished it—and him. Scott left Rosewood because he felt like nobody. You drove him away."

He flinched at that concise playback. "We agree on something, I see. Believe me, I have wished many times that I had been a better big brother to Scott. Right now, I'd give anything to tell him that, but I don't know where he is." He hadn't meant to say that much. On the other hand, the admission might appeal to her emotions and sway her to his side.

"Neither do I," Wendy said. "He left here about three weeks ago, and as far as I know, he didn't even tell Quentin Whitefoot, his closest friend, where he was going."

Eric knew all about Quentin. He leaned over to his bedside table, opened the drawer, and held up an envelope. "This letter brought me here to Shadow Ridge. It's from Quentin Whitefoot."

"What's he doing writing to you? How does he even know who you are?"

"Scott told Quentin to write to me if anything happened to him." He had her attention now. He tried to break it to her gently. "Scott didn't leave Shadow Ridge willingly, Wendy. Something did happen to him."

"What are you saying?"

"All I know from the letter I got a few days back is that three weeks ago Scott had some sort of accident and then disappeared. That's why he hasn't been seen since." Eric held out the letter.

She took it and skimmed the contents. Her face went white. "Accident? Missing? That's impossible." She frowned. "Joe told me he had left town."

"Joe? Who's Joe?"

"Joseph Chandler. He's one of the two doctors here. I guess you haven't met him yet."

"Young, looks like an ex-hippie, long, straggly hair, dirty sneakers, and wears a stethoscope around his neck?"

Wendy nodded. "That's him," she said. "And despite his casual appearance, he *is* a good doctor."

"Joe Chandler's skills really don't concern me, but if he's involved somehow in Scott's disappearance, I'm very interested. You say he told you Scott had left town?"

"He did, but he was probably just telling me what he'd heard. News travels like a brushfire in Shadow Ridge. He could have heard it anywhere."

Eric took out a small notepad and pen from his bedside table drawer and wrote something. In response to Wendy's sharp look of suspicion, he smiled benignly. "I'm just making myself a note to talk to Dr. Chandler."

Wendy said nothing for a few moments, and Eric suspected she was trying to process what he had told her.

"Scott was in trouble, and I didn't help him," she said in a tight, sad voice.

Eric ached to draw her close and offer comfort, but he didn't dare. "You had no idea, Wendy. How could you have known if he didn't tell you? All he told Quentin Whitefoot was to get in touch with me if anything happened to him. Scott must have known he was in danger. He wouldn't have wanted to involve his friends in it. He must have cared a great deal about you."

When she looked up, unshed tears filled her beautiful eyes. At that moment, no matter what trouble his little brother was in, Eric wished he were Scott.

Sensing that she was softening, he came to the point. "It's obvious Scott meant a great deal to you, Wendy, and he could use your help now. Everyone I've talked to here seems to believe you can do anything but walk on water. I'd like that kind of person on our side."

"Is this what you didn't want to be distracted from?" she asked.

Eric nodded helplessly. "I'm afraid we got off on the wrong foot. I can't deny there's chemistry between us, but I didn't come here to find love, just my brother," he said bluntly. "Can we start again—as friends, with a mutual goal of finding Scott?

Wendy quickly corrected him. "We're merely acquaintances."

"I rescued you in the fog. You've taken care of me here. Doesn't that make us friends?"

"Excuse me, but you almost ran me over in the fog. I rescued myself. And the entire staff is taking care of you here," she pointed out.

Eric smiled contritely. "You're right, of course."

"If I help you, it will be solely for Scott's benefit," she said firmly.

"He must mean a lot to you. In fact, many sources told me that you and Scott were . . . an item," Eric said, hoping she would elaborate on the nature of her relationship with his brother.

Wendy chuckled but did not enlighten him. "This is a small town, Mr. Tremaine. People have few pastimes—a little TV and occasionally a very old movie at the town hall. Matchmaking is the local hobby. Rest assured that, because of all the questions you've asked about me, the whole town will have *us* paired up by noon tomorrow and engaged by the weekend. And we don't even like each other. Does that answer your question?"

He shook his head. "Not really. Besides, I do like you."

"Get over it." She marched out, and Eric was relieved to see her back in fighting form.

Chapter Four

Quentin Whitefoot was a hard man to find. Wendy tried his house, but neither he nor his pregnant wife, Opal, was there. Quentin could be almost anywhere. In the end, she bumped into him, literally, at the grocery store. Their carts collided in the canned-goods aisle.

"Whoa, Wendy. Slow down. Where's the fire?" Quentin steadied her with a firm grip.

"Quent! I was just at your house looking for you. . . ." Her voice faltered when she looked at his shopping cart.

He laughed at her expression. "Opal got another craving— one of her last, I hope," he explained, shrugging. There were several tins of sardines, a box of soda crackers, and a fresh salmon in the basket.

"That's an awful lot of salt for a pregnant woman," she said.

"That's what I thought," he said. "But I dare you to tell her."

Wendy laughed at the idea that Quentin was afraid of his petite wife. "Other than the cravings, how's she doing?" Wendy walked beside him toward the checkout.

"Feeling like a blue whale. She's only got another month,

but it might as well be a year." He nodded in the general direction of the clinic. "She's at the doctor's now. I'm picking her up when I'm done here."

Wendy paid for her supplies and waited for him to get through the line. As they were leaving the store, she said, "Actually, I wanted to talk to you about—"

He finished her sentence. "Eric Tremaine?" He smiled at the face she made. "He told me you'd be asking. I saw him and Horace this morning after he got out of the hospital."

"Are you sure he's who he says he is, Quentin? I mean, had you ever met him before?"

"You sure are suspicious, aren't you, Wendy? Scott told me about his older brother and gave me his address, and Eric showed me a picture of the two of them. I'm satisfied."

Wendy still had more questions than answers about Eric Tremaine. She had hoped to talk to Quentin before Eric could, but no such luck. Apparently Quentin had fallen under the Eric Tremaine spell, like everyone else who came into contact with the man from Seattle.

They had been walking toward the clinic, and as they neared it, a stunningly beautiful, doe-eyed native girl approached with the typical waddle of late pregnancy.

"Hello, Wendy," she said with a friendly smile.

"Hi, Opal. You're glowing, as always. How are you doing? What did the doctor say today?"

Opal sighed. "The same as Quentin. 'Be patient.' Wendy, you'll still be my nurse when the time comes, won't you?"

"Of course," Wendy assured her. She looked at the young aboriginal girl, barely seventeen, and she felt a wave of compassion. She could not imagine having a baby at that age. She had been so young at seventeen, so naïve. She knew that girls grew up faster in this culture, but her heart still went out to the young ones who became mothers before they had finished their teens. "If I'm not already at the hospital when you go into labor, call me, day or night."

Opal looked relieved. "Thank you. You are a good friend."

She nudged her husband in the ribs. "Quentin, invite Wendy for supper."

"Of course, my muffin. Wendy, will you come for supper tonight?" He looked both ways and leaned close, as if conspiring with her. "A certain mutual acquaintance—who shall remain nameless—is coming to discuss a certain delicate matter, and he said you should be there."

"But I wanted to talk to you alone, without *him* there," Wendy protested.

Quentin helped Opal into his pickup, shut her door, and walked around to his side. "It's better with all of us there. Teamwork." He climbed into the truck and slammed the door. "Come at six."

"But—" Her objection was lost in the squeal of tires and the spitting gravel Quentin left behind him.

No sooner had Wendy reached the Whitefoots' A-frame log cabin at 5:30, hoping to discuss matters with Quentin before Eric arrived, than big raindrops began pelting her. She bolted up the porch steps and almost fell through the door when it opened unexpectedly.

Eric caught her before she landed. "I see you got here early too. Good thing you missed the rain," he said softly, his lips only millimeters from her cheek. He seemed reluctant to release her.

For a brief second, Wendy's mind stopped functioning. Then she rallied, pulling away from him and wondering why she hadn't noticed his pickup. "I thought we were supposed to meet here at six," she muttered crossly. It was even harder to deal with the effect he had on her without her uniform and her professional objectivity. She needed to keep control of the situation.

Wendy shook off her cumbersome gum boots and hung up her jacket. She had hoped to arrive before Eric, but apparently he'd had the same idea. He hung his jacket up beside hers, revealing that he had arrived but a moment earlier.

"Do I detect a little hostility?" Quentin asked with a big

grin on his face. He greeted his guests and waved them into the main room of his cabin.

Although not much taller than Wendy, Quentin was stocky. His grin now contradicted his intimidating appearance, something that had come in handy when two young punks thought they would scare Wendy one night when she walking home alone. Quentin had happened along, sized up the situation, and scared the boys off. Wendy's gratitude for his timely intervention had evolved into a comfortable friendship.

"You're both so early that Opal and I can be in bed by nine." He chuckled.

Wendy had been to this cabin many times. It reminded her of an alpine ski lodge, warm, inviting, and quaint. The fire in the hearth burned low, and she was glad; the room temperature must be a hundred. Opal already sat in her favorite recliner with her feet propped up. Wendy was pleased to note that her legs were not puffy.

Quentin secured their other recliner, positioned beside Opal's for optimum TV watching. "Come on, people, take a load off. Supper isn't for a while yet; let's visit."

In the small cabin, with barely room for one love seat and the two recliners, Eric watched Wendy glare at the love seat, and his heart sank. He could practically see her recoil as she calculated how close to him she would have to sit. Would she ever forgive him? Would he ever have a chance to make up for his mistake?

At that moment, Opal vacated her chair to check on her supper preparations, and Wendy followed to help.

Eric noticed a table with aboriginal carvings in a corner and wandered over to it. "You do some excellent carving, Quentin," he said. "May I take a closer look at these?"

"Of course," Quentin said, looking very pleased. "This is what I do for a living." He joined Eric at the workbench. On it were totems of all sizes and shapes as well as silver jewelry—rings, necklaces, and pins—all carved in the distinctive animal shapes of the Pacific Coast natives. "Here, hold this one." Quentin held up a black totem six inches high. "Feel how smooth it is?"

"And heavy," Eric said, surprised. He turned it over in his hand. "What's it made of?"

"Argillite. It's a slate rock found on the Queen Charlottes," Quentin told him. "Only the Haida chiefs know where to find it, and because it's so rare, it's also valuable."

Eric put the totem down. "Then how did you manage to get hold of it?"

"I am Haida," Quentin said proudly. "My uncle is the best carver on the Islands and one of the few who knows where the argillite deposit is. I can get it whenever I need it." He held a small lump of black stone and dropped it into Eric's hand. "This is what it looks like before we carve it." The stone had the appearance of coal, except it was as smooth as butter.

"Exactly how valuable is this slate?" Eric asked.

"This six-inch totem would sell for about five hundred dollars in Vancouver," Quentin said.

Eric whistled softly.

From the kitchen, Wendy announced that supper was ready, breaking up the discussion. The men joined the two women in the spacious room designated as kitchen and dining room. Quentin plunked himself down in his usual chair, inviting Eric and Wendy to sit opposite each other. Opal brought the plates to the table, each one already filled with smoked salmon, peas, and boiled potatoes.

As soon as she sat down, Quentin said, "Dig in, folks," and proceeded to do exactly that.

Opal suddenly grabbed her side and cried out.

"Are you all right?" Wendy asked, jumping up. She wondered if she would have to call for the ambulance and turned to Opal's husband. "Quentin?"

He looked up but continued pouring water into each glass. "This happens all the time," he said calmly.

"I'm fine," Opal gasped. "It's just a kick. This is a very strong baby," she said with a grimace. Quentin grinned from ear to ear as if he were personally and completely responsible for his baby's strength.

Men are so conceited, she thought. "Must be a girl," she deliberately said, which sparked a heated discussion about which sex was the stronger.

After that icebreaker, conversation at the table flowed smoothly. Eric asked Quentin more about his carving, and Wendy and Opal discussed babies. Wendy enjoyed herself more than she had expected. She had dreaded the prospect of a social occasion with Eric. She really didn't want to get to know him. She certainly didn't want to like him—Scott's tyrannical big brother. But she had to admit, Eric was the perfect dinner guest. Natural and easygoing, he laughed at Quentin's jokes, was solicitous over Opal. The couple had readily fallen under his usual spell.

When the meal was over, Wendy insisted on doing the dishes, and she shooed Opal into the other room to sit down. The men didn't even pretend to be interested in helping. Secretly, she was relieved to be away from Eric. Throughout the meal, she had been too aware of his intense, masculine presence. Her eyes had strayed in his direction far too often. Worse, Quentin had caught her at it several times, and she knew he was bursting to say something.

Someone came into the kitchen. Assuming it was her hostess, Wendy said, "Now, Opal, I told you to just go and relax."

"And she is being very obedient," said Eric from behind her.

Wendy whipped around. At the sight of him filling her vision, her heart missed a beat. She hated feeling this vulnerable to a man, especially when he looked so . . . so unaffected by her presence.

"I thought I could help you, so we can get down to the business of why we're here." He found a towel and picked up a plate to dry. "That is, in case you've forgotten. It's about Scott."

She almost dropped the plate in her hand. "I could never forget *Scott,*" she said, with the emphasis on his brother's name. "*You,* on the other hand . . ."

"Now, now, Wendy, let's not say things we'll regret later." He dried another plate and began a pile on the table. "Quentin told me you have doubts about my relationship to Scott." He put down his dish towel. "I don't think you believe a word I've said. Here. Look." Eric took out his wallet, pulled out a snapshot, and held it in front of her face. "Here's a photo of Scott and me." The picture showed a teenaged Scott, perhaps sixteen, with longer hair and sideburns. He was standing rather stiffly beside Eric, who looked much older.

He tugged out some cards. "Here's my driver's license, my bank card, and a credit card. Satisfied?"

"That photo looks pretty old. And it doesn't prove anything. Don't you have something that identifies you as brothers?"

"I haven't seen Scott in a couple of years. This was the most recent photo I could find with both of us together. It's only about four years old."

"Sorry to say, you haven't aged very well."

"Ouch." He pretended to check himself for wounds. "It's okay. Nothing vital was hit, just my ego. You know, Wendy, I wondered why, with your beauty and intelligence, you weren't having to beat men off with sticks, but it's now clear—you scare them away with sarcasm, condescension, and the perfect put-down. If you're aiming to stay single for a good long time, I'd say your chances are excellent." He gave up all pretense of drying dishes and waited for her reaction.

Wendy was stunned that he had actually confronted her like that. Most men were running scared by now. None had ever challenged her. The gloves were off. *Good.* She would be equally blunt. "I see my plan is working," she told him, putting the last dish in the drainer and turning to face him. "And you catch on fast. I do intend to remain single—forever, actually. And since we are being so candid, I regret signing on to help you find Scott, much as I want to know where he is. All I know is, you are probably the last person he wants to see and maybe even the one responsible for whatever went wrong for him."

"Are you blaming me for what's happened to Scott?"

"If the shoe fits." Wendy raised her voice a few notches.

"Are you two finished arguing yet?" Quentin called from the living room, interrupting them. "Opal is getting tired, and we go to bed early around here. Come on out, and let's talk."

Eric seemed as relieved as Wendy at Quentin's intervention. She was glad to see that Quentin and Opal were snuggled up on the sofa. She sat in Opal's recliner, grateful for even a little distance from Eric.

"Hush, Quent, it's only seven o'clock," Opal contradicted, poking him in the ribs. The room, so warm before supper, now felt a bit chilly. Quentin had built up the fire, but its warmth had not quite reached Wendy yet. She felt chilled to the bone, and it was not entirely because of the room temperature.

Quentin whispered something to Opal, and she went out to the kitchen and started rattling dishes.

"Now," Quentin said as though he were opening parliament, "let's talk."

Eric leaned forward, hands clenched. "Your letter was pretty vague and sketchy, Quentin. Fill in the details, will you?"

Quentin unfurled his length and crossed his hands behind his head. "I'll start with just before Scott came here from Vancouver. He was working for a magazine—*Indian Art,* I think he called it. They sent him up the coast to write about Haida argillite. Scott said he got interested in it in Vancouver. Anyway, he came here just after New Year's and looked me up. He had actually heard of me." Quentin's face was a picture of wonder. "He asked me questions about everything I did, especially about the totems. He was fascinated by the argillite. He even asked me to take him to Slate Mountain."

"What about this 'accident' you wrote me about?"

"I'm getting to that. For a month, Scott practically lived in our house. Then he started hanging out at the pool hall—and with Wendy." He winked broadly at her. "Eh, Wendy? When I did see him a couple of weeks before he disappeared, it was short and to the point. He told me that there was an ugly side to the story he was writing and that he might be getting himself into trouble. He gave me your address, Eric, and asked me to get in touch with you if anything happened to him. He also told me not to trust the cops."

Opal returned from the kitchen with a tray full of steaming mugs of coffee. Gratefully, Wendy wrapped both hands around hers for the warmth. She felt so cold. Quentin's terse account of the events had brought home to her the reality that Scott was in trouble, serious trouble. She glanced at Eric. Whatever differences they had with each other paled in comparison to Scott's welfare. His glance met hers, and she thought she read a similar thought on his face. Eric looked ten years older now than when he had arrived. Despite her desire to hate him, she felt a pang of sympathy for him.

"Are you all right, Eric?" Opal asked, as he heaped sugar into his cup.

"I'm okay, Opal. Thanks for the coffee. It smells awfully good." Like Wendy, Eric cradled the mug with both hands. "Please go on, Quentin."

"Right. Well, long story short, Scott somehow got mixed up in something dangerous, and whatever it was, he didn't tell me. I didn't know what to do."

"And the accident?" prompted Eric.

Quentin sat forward. "I was walking on the beach near Gull Point the night before Scott supposedly left Shadow Ridge, and I heard a car up on the road. It's a pretty steep drop from the road in that area. I heard sounds of arguing, but it was too far away for me to tell who was talking or make out any words. Then someone yelled, as if he'd fallen over the embankment, and a few minutes later I heard a car drive away. I couldn't make out much with just moonlight. I heard moaning, so I ran toward it."

He took a deep breath and rubbed his eyes as if to make that night clearer in his mind's eye. "By the time I got there, the moaning had stopped, but in the moonlight I saw a body. When I got close, I saw it was Scott, and he wasn't moving." Quentin paused briefly. "Now comes the strange part," he continued, his expression displaying his bewilderment.

A log suddenly crumpled in the hearth, and sparks flew up like fireworks. Wendy flinched.

"What?" Eric whispered. He was as pale as death itself. Perspiration glistened on his forehead.

"Well, he had rolled down the cliff, and he was definitely out cold. And his leg looked off-kilter somehow. I knew I had to get him help, but I didn't dare move him in case he'd broken his neck." Quentin glanced at Wendy. "I learned that from *North of 60,*" he told her with a wry grin.

She managed a smile. "Who says television is a wasteland? So you called for help?"

"Trouble was, I have no cell phone, so I had to leave him there to get help. I ran all the way home and called the hospital. It couldn't have been more than fifteen or twenty minutes later. Dr. Joe came out, and when we got to the place"—Quentin shrugged his broad shoulders, puzzled—"there was no Scott. Nothing. Dr. Joe was pretty mad, I'll tell you. Accused me of being drunk—threatened to report me to the Mounties."

"Joe Chandler?" Wendy asked, incredulous.

"Yeah, the one and only. He was not happy to be out there looking for someone who wasn't there. You can guess how I felt. I couldn't imagine Scott getting up and walking away, not the way he had looked when I left him."

Eric was silent, staring into the fire for several moments. No one else spoke. Finally he said, "If Scott couldn't leave under his own power, then someone else must have come along and taken him away."

"I couldn't stay with him and go for help at the same time," Quentin said, sounding defensive.

"Of course not, Quentin," Wendy assured him. "You did the only thing you could. The question is, who took him and where?"

"That's what Horace and I came here to find out," Eric said, rubbing his forehead. "I just don't know where to start." He looked around the room as if hoping for the answer. He was beginning to look pasty, Wendy thought. *Almost as bad as the night we met.*

"Eric has had enough, Quent," Opal said, poking her husband in the ribs again. "Let him go home to sleep. You can talk more tomorrow."

"That's a good idea, Opal," Wendy said, uncurling from her chair and stretching her limbs.

"Eric, why don't you drop Wendy off? It's pretty dark out there," Quentin said, grinning at Wendy, as if he knew she would hate the idea. He knew her well, she thought.

"Sure, no problem." He stood up, but his legs threatened to buckle. He reached out and grabbed Wendy for support.

Eric's touch sent a thrill coursing through her. She only hoped he didn't notice her quickened breathing. She wanted to be indifferent to him, but her body betrayed her.

"It's just that pesky chemistry, Wendy. Nothing to worry about," he whispered, as if he knew exactly what she felt.

Which was so annoying.

"Here, lean on me, Eric," Quentin told him, grabbing his other arm.

"I'm partial to Wendy's healing touch," he said with an exaggerated leer. He pulled himself upright. "Really, I'm okay now, thanks. I sat too long, and my leg fell asleep, that's all."

"Thanks for the wonderful supper, Opal," Wendy said, getting into her coat. She slipped out to the porch, put her boots on, and waited for Eric. She planned to tell him she would plunge into the moonless night by herself.

Stepping out of the cabin and into the complete darkness, Eric asked, "Wendy, where are you?"

"I'm right here. Where are—ouch!"

"What happened?" Eric groped about and finally touched her sleeve. He pulled her close to him and put an arm around her.

She was no fool. It was too dark for her to walk the mile

back to town. She would have to let Eric drive her. "I scraped my ankle on a rock. It's nothing. Where's your truck?"

"Right here."

She heard him open the pickup door. Light from the cab illuminated the immediate area. Ignoring her protest, Eric helped her into the passenger seat. He shut her door, went around to the driver's side, and climbed in beside her. As soon as he was settled behind the wheel, he turned on the dome light. Reaching across her, he opened the glove compartment and pulled out a first-aid kit. He smelled of wood smoke, coffee, and some intangible male aroma. A sudden longing filled her. She couldn't explain it or put it into words. She just felt . . . needy.

He turned to her just then. "Excuse me," he said. She lowered her eyes so he wouldn't see what was there.

"Let's see your ankle."

"I told you, it's nothing. Let's just go. I'll be out of your hair in a few minutes."

"I'll decide when I want you out of my hair. Let me see your ankle."

This is ridiculous, thought Wendy. It would take longer to argue about it than just to let him see the foot. She slipped off her torn boot, then bent her knee across her other leg. There was blood on her white sock, and she pulled it off.

As he opened the kit, she said quickly, "It's just a scratch." She could see the swelling around her ankle and a jagged but superficial cut. It stung badly, exposed to the air.

"Take it from me, scratches can be deadly." He smiled. After daubing cold disinfectant all over it, he patted it dry with sterile gauze. When he was satisfied it was clean, he put a wide plaster on it. His touch was sending quivers of electricity along her skin.

"I'm surprised you know first aid," she said, replacing her sock and boot, both of which were now ruined.

He put the kit down between them and turned off the dome light. "You really mean, why did I let my own cut get so bad that I had to be hospitalized, don't you?"

"Well, yes, I am wondering."

After starting the engine, he slowly maneuvered the narrow path down to the main road. "Working a horse ranch has forced me to learn first-aid essentials and that a simple scratch can become infected in no time." He turned to face her. "My only excuse is that finding Scott seemed more important than trying to treat a cut I couldn't even reach." He turned right at the highway.

Wendy said nothing for several moments. She thought about how much her life had changed in barely forty-eight hours. Her comfortable, secure little world had turned upside down. Before hearing Quentin's story, she might have been able to convince herself that nothing bad had happened to Scott, that he had just moved on, but now she could no longer believe that. Scott was missing. No one knew why or who was behind it. She glanced over at Eric. He was deep in thought himself.

"Do you still want my help to find Scott?" she asked.

There was a pause, and she was suddenly afraid he would say no.

"Only if you want to."

That was a change from the evening before, when he had practically begged her to help him. He had also told her he liked her. That had probably changed too, since their exchange in Opal's kitchen. "Scott was my friend," she said, and suddenly tears were streaming down her face. "I have to help," she said with a hiccup.

Eric handed her a tissue and let her cry. When she seemed under control, he said, "Do you really believe it's my fault Scott was hurt and has disappeared?"

"After what Quent said, how can I? I just said that because you . . . well, you seem to rub me the wrong way, that's all." Eric massaged his forehead. Wendy felt ashamed. She wasn't in the habit of speaking her mind so freely, especially to someone she hardly knew. "I'm sorry," she said. Not only was he worried about Scott, but he was still convalescing from a serious infection that could keep most people bedridden for days.

"I'm sorry about what I said too." He turned toward her, and she glimpsed a grin on his face. "Can we start over again? Friends? Acquaintances? Partners?"

"I will do everything in my power to help you find Scott," she told him, tears falling silently down her cheeks. "And I don't know what we are," she added, a forlorn note to her voice. "I guess partners is a good place to start."

"Scott is lucky to have such a loyal friend." Eric pulled up at the nurses' residence door. "I realize what a sacrifice it is for you to work with me, but I'm not your enemy, Wendy. Nor Scott's. I hope you will see that one day." He leaned across her to open her door. "I'll be in touch," he told her. She jumped out, and as soon as she shut the door, he sped off.

Wendy entered the residence and was glad not to have to answer any questions about her evening. She went straight to bed but slept little that night.

Chapter Five

Over the next few days, Wendy saw little of Eric and Horace. She began to wonder if Eric had decided she was more a liability than an asset. Small-town gossip being what it was, she was well aware that the American visitors had already become minor celebrities in Shadow Ridge. Not that anyone knew why they had come, she discovered. Eric was playing it close to the vest, and nobody asked questions because no one wanted to answer any.

"Maybe we could incorporate Eric Tremaine into a skit at our Spring Social," Mrs. Welsh remarked two days later at the planning meeting. Wendy couldn't remember another time when an ex-patient had been invited to participate in one of the hospital events. It was a mark of how well Eric had wheedled his way into their circle. So why hadn't she seen him since they had been to the Whitefoot house?

"Sounds good to me," Janet said. "Can we put him into tights?" she said with a leer.

"And maybe he could sing something just for you, Janet, like 'The Impossible Dream.' "

"Very funny, Wendy."

"Can Eric sing?" asked Connie innocently.

"He's so good-looking, does it matter?" laughed Janet, winking meaningfully at Wendy.

"He's awfully nice," added Connie, much to everyone's surprise. Connie was another one who played it close to the vest.

"I'm sure you'll all come up with something he can do," Wendy said, annoyed at the way the conversation had gone off on this tangent.

"Count on it." Janet winked.

By the following Thursday afternoon, Wendy had finished her shift and was looking forward to a long weekend off. She and Janet had decided to go to the movie playing at the town hall that evening. The film was old by Vancouver standards but a first-run feature in Shadow Ridge. Most of the town showed up, no matter what the film was, just for the evening out.

To Wendy's surprise, Janet stopped by the police station and picked up Constable Ganzer. "Wendy, you know John Ganzer, don't you? Since he's relatively new to the area, I thought he might enjoy some Shadow Ridge social life."

"Hello, Miss Hunt." He nodded politely. His offhand greeting gave Wendy no clue whether he remembered her from the night he had come to arrest the drunks Dr. Thomas had sewn up at the hospital. He had an air of distance about him, as if he lived on an island quite apart from the rest of the world. In a big city, no one would notice. Here, it stood out.

"Call her Wendy, John. No one is that formal here."

He smiled, but it was not particularly friendly. "I guess I'm really still a big-city cop. You keep a distance with people till you get to know them."

"There you go, Wendy. You and John already have a lot in common," Janet said.

"Quite a good turnout tonight," Wendy remarked, not sure what Janet was playing at.

"Does everybody show up at these movies?" John asked, gazing around the room. It was no mere glance; he scanned every

detail. Wendy could almost see his inner wheels whir as he cata-
logued everybody. Before Janet could answer his question, he
said, "Excuse me," and headed for someone in a far corner.

As soon as he had gone, Wendy turned on Janet. "What was
that crack about having so much in common with John Ganzer
all about? Is this another one of your setups?"

Janet laughed. "I just said that to get your goat. It's too easy,
like shooting fish in a barrel. John is for me, by the way. He's
got hidden talents." She waggled her eyebrows.

"I don't think I want to know," Wendy said. She watched the
Mountie circulate. "You'll never lose him in a crowd, though,
will you?"

"How was I to know he'd wear his red serge?" Janet shrugged.
"I think he's out to get someone. See how he's grilling that man?
Something's afoot, Watson," she said, with her best Sherlock
Holmes accent. "Well, look who just came in—no, don't look."

The warning came too late. Joe Chandler spotted Wendy
looking at him and made a beeline over to her. Connie, with a
tight grip on Eric Tremaine, followed right behind him.

"Goody, all my favorite people are here," Janet muttered
under her breath.

Wendy reacted to Eric's presence exactly the way she hoped
she wouldn't. Her heart picked up speed, and her breath caught
in her throat. Seeing him with Connie, who had just admitted to
liking him, was a surprise. Maybe Connie was the reason Eric
hadn't contacted her all week.

Had the two become an item? He had made it clear to
Wendy that a relationship was the last thing he wanted. Of
course, a bolt of love could foul up the best-laid plans of mice
and men. Could he have fallen so hard for Connie that he had
been unable to resist her? As Wendy recalled how easily
everyone in Eric's vicinity fell under his spell, it seemed possible that he could have swept Connie off her feet. Or had he
merely found a different and prettier helper in his search for
Scott? She wasn't jealous, she told herself, just curious.

Joe had said something and seemed to be waiting for Wendy's

response. She had to ask him to repeat it. "Where have you been all week? I've called a few times, but you're always out." His voice was loud enough to cause the closest bystanders to turn and look at them.

Before she could phrase her response, Eric and Connie joined them. Connie stayed close to Eric, holding on to his arm like a lifeline.

Eric smiled at everyone, but his glance stopped at Wendy. "How nice to see you all here. It's like being in the hospital again." Everyone laughed, which eased the tension.

The lights dimmed, and they all scrambled for seats. Wendy paused, waiting for Joe to sit. She would then sit as far away from him as possible. The little talk they had had the other day seemed to have gone in one ear and out the other. She had told Joe as plainly as possible that she was not interested in a romantic relationship with him. What more would it take, she wondered.

Eric leaned over and whispered, "I've recently heard something that could be significant. If I can walk you home after the movie, we can talk."

"What about Connie? You came with her."

He looked puzzled. "No, I didn't. I came alone. She was standing outside the door, and as soon as I arrived, she offered to escort me in. I think she's trying to make someone jealous."

Well, it worked. Aloud, Wendy said, "Oh?"

Eric nodded. "Yup. My guess would be Dr. Chandler, because as soon as she saw him, she practically dragged me over here. But that's just a guess." He took her elbow and guided her to a seat. "Here, we'd better sit down. The movie's starting."

She nodded. Connie and Joe? When the movie credits finally rolled an hour and a half later, she couldn't have told anyone the plot of the kung fu action thriller. She had been thinking of Connie and Joe. Eric and Connie. Wendy and Eric.

When the lights went up, Wendy informed Janet she would

be walking home with Eric, making it quite clear that it was to discuss something important.

"Go ahead, but you're not fooling anyone with that line. Anyway, I was just wondering how I was going to ditch you to get some alone time with John. Problem solved. Have fun."

Eric took longer to extricate himself from Connie's grasp, but eventually he pulled her over to where Joe was standing alone. Wendy saw the two men talking. Then Eric put Connie's hand on Joe's arm and walked away smiling. Neither of them looked as pleased as Eric.

"Alone at last," he chuckled after he and Wendy had left the hall. "And a full moon to guide us home." Despite the romantic moonlight, he made no attempt to take her hand, put an arm around her shoulder, or in any way touch her. *What a relief.*

"What's the big news? I was on pins and needles all through the movie, waiting for it to end."

He turned to study her in the moonlight. "From where I was sitting, you looked riveted to the screen, absolutely enthralled. For the life of me, I can't figure out those martial arts movies. They're not heavy on plot, are they? Have you missed me this week?"

"Missed you? Has it been a whole week? Goodness, time flies."

"Well, I've missed you," he said with a smile. "Although God only knows why, after the slings and arrows you've let fly at me since we met."

"The sympathy train just left the station, Eric. And you've slung your share of arrows too. Let's just say we're even and move on, shall we? Now, enough small talk. What's going on? Have you found Scott?"

Eric chuckled. "You are refreshingly honest, although heartless. My news isn't about Scott, at least not directly. Sorry if I built your hopes up. I forgot that you love him and hate me." He paused. Did he want her to deny that statement?

It would be easier if she was in love with Scott, but she

wasn't. It would be simpler if she hated Eric. But it was more complicated than that. There was also this pesky chemistry that was, she was disappointed to discover, still very much in play.

"Moving on, then." He cleared his throat. "I was at Quentin's this morning, and he told me something interesting. You remember he said his uncle is one of the few Haidas who know how to access the argillite in this Slate Mountain?" She nodded. "Quentin's uncle told him that there has been unauthorized mining of the argillite—in other words, someone is stealing it. Even the RCMP have been investigating it. I wonder if Scott found out something about that."

"That makes sense," she said. "And if he found out who was stealing the argillite, they wouldn't like it. They just might feel inclined to push him off a cliff to silence him. Did *they* go down and get him and . . ." She couldn't say *finish him off*.

"I followed that line of thinking too, Wendy, but I can't help feeling that Scott is still alive, somehow, somewhere. Maybe it's just wishful thinking."

"If he is out there, I hope he's getting some expert medical attention. From what Quent said about that night, I'd say that along with a serious head injury, Scott's leg was broken, and maybe a few other bones."

Eric looked at her as if she had discovered fire. "Wendy, I think you're on to something."

"I am?"

"Yes," he said, excited now. "Let's suppose that whoever took Scott away didn't do it to finish the job—I know that's what you're thinking. What if someone besides both Quentin and the bad guys saw Scott fall?" He fell silent for several moments. "Scott would have needed to be taken away. All we have to do is find out who and where."

Presently, Wendy said, "Here we are. I'm home."

Eric looked up. "Already?"

"Already. I'm off tomorrow for a couple of days. What can I do to help find Scott? Interviews, interrogations, bone-crunching?"

Eric looked startled for a second. Then he grinned. "You are quite the friend in need, Wendy Hunt." He chucked. "No bone-crunching just yet. I'll let you know."

As she started up the residence steps, he said, "Wendy, wait." Something in his tone made her stop and turn around to face him. "Horace and I are heading home tomorrow. We've done all we can from here."

Wendy felt as if she'd been sucker-punched. He was leaving? So soon? "Now?" she asked incredulously. "We've just had a breakthrough—you can't leave now." He said nothing, just stared at her with something like sadness in his face. "But the argillite robbers—we should follow that up." She sounded desperate, even to herself. Shouldn't she be glad he was leaving? Isn't that what she had wanted since he arrived?

"We'll check a few hospitals on the way to Vancouver to see if we find any trace of Scott's having been there, but I have to say, it's probably a long shot. Other than that, I don't know what more we can do here. The RCMP are investigating the argillite matter." His voice became husky. "I've heard they always get their man."

It was a reminder of when they had met. Wendy had been suspicious of him, reluctant to be near him. Now she was shamelessly begging him to stay? *Oh, how the mighty have fallen,* she moaned inwardly. Despite all her best defenses, no-trespassing signs, and electric fences around her heart, Eric Tremaine had managed to slip inside before she had even realized it.

Wendy was standing on the first step. Eric moved closer until they were eye to eye. "Thanks for all you've done, Wendy. I couldn't have asked for better care when I was sick." Wendy hated good-byes. They were awkward, full of clichés. On the other hand, this was the one she had wanted for a week. Why, then, were her eyes tearing up? "I'll be sure to let you know how it all turns out," Eric continued. "Or, God willing, Scott will. I hope I have the chance to return your kindness when you come to my neck of the woods."

Another cliché. Why even think she would ever go to Rose-wood? "What . . ." She couldn't finish that thought because Eric pulled her close and kissed her. This time he kissed her on the lips, a tender, gentle, good-bye kiss, one that lingered there long after he was out of sight.

Wendy wandered up to the kitchen. She poured herself some hot chocolate and sat at the window looking out into the darkness. From the beginning, Eric had posed a threat to her safe, heart-whole world. She should be relieved that he was going—it was none too soon. Why, then, did she feel so bereft? After an hour of fruitless soul-searching, she went to bed.

A loud knocking on her bedroom door the following morning forced Wendy back to consciousness. Slowly, she surfaced from her dreamless slumber and recognized Connie's voice.

"Come in," she called, her voice husky with sleep.

Connie came in and plopped down on Wendy's bed. "Guess who's downstairs asking—no, demanding—to see you?"

Wendy squinted at Connie. "I can't imagine. What time is it, anyway?"

"It's six-thirty. Eric Tremaine's here."

Wendy's eyes flew open.

"He said he'd come up and get you himself if you weren't down there in fifteen minutes."

"Oh, he did, did he?" Wendy stared at Connie's beaming chocolate brown eyes. "Why are you so happy?"

Connie shook her head in disbelief. "You really don't know, do you?"

"No, I guess I don't."

Connie jumped to her feet and sighed like a teacher with a slow learner. "If you have Eric Tremaine, then you can let Joe go," she said, as if she were speaking to a child—a particularly dense one.

Wendy sat up, pushed her covers back, and scrounged around on the floor for her slippers. It gave her time to think. "Connie, I don't want Joe. We're just co-workers. I had no idea . . .

I mean, you've never seemed interested in him—or anyone else, for that matter—since I've known you." Wendy scratched her head. "Although you looked pretty cozy with Eric last night."

Connie sighed again. "That was to make Joe jealous. It didn't work. The whole way home, he fumed because you went with Eric, and he was stuck with me." Her voice faltered, and Wendy felt a twinge of pity. Eric had been right on the money.

Sympathy evaporated quickly at Connie's next words. "Don't deny you've been leading Joe on ever since you came here," she said coldly. "I haven't had a chance with him. You don't need two boyfriends. Let him go, so I can have him." She slammed Wendy's door on her way out.

Connie's jealous, cockeyed thinking confirmed Wendy's hypothesis: love, or whatever you called it, turned intelligent, rational people into idiots. There was nothing she could do about Connie's malaise. Eric was waiting downstairs.

As her treacherous heart sped up at that thought, Wendy knew she would have to work hard to keep her emotions in check. *Chemistry,* Eric had called it. He was right; these feelings were caused solely by a surge of hormones sent out by the pituitary gland that activated the autonomic nervous system, resulting in physical responses: rapid heart rate, sweaty palms, quickened breathing. *Chemistry, that's all.*

Dressing quickly in navy sweat pants and beige sweatshirt, she took a deep breath and went downstairs. At the sight of Eric waiting for her in the hallway, her breath caught. *It's only a chemical reaction,* she told herself as she reached him. "What are you doing here?" Her voice sounded too breathy. She cleared her throat. "You said you were leaving." That was better, more normal.

"It's Horace."

"What's happened? Is he sick?"

"No, he's disappeared. He went somewhere last evening, while I was at the movie. He didn't leave a note and never came back last night. I'm sure something's happened to him." Eric took her arm and led her out of the building. "Walk with me, please. I can't stand to be doing nothing."

She managed to grab her jacket off the hook on the way out. Apparently she had no choice but to be dragged out into the cold morning. "Would you mind telling me where we're going?" she said, trying to keep up with his long strides.

"Horace is missing. I'm going to the police."

"You don't need me for that," she protested, stopping in her tracks.

"I thought it might be helpful if a respected citizen went with me," he told her, taking her arm and pulling her along again. "Besides, this may have something to do with Scott's disappearance, and you said you wanted to help, right?"

"Just so long as I don't 'distract' you," she muttered crossly, marching ahead of him.

He grabbed her arm. "Just for the record, Wendy Hunt, you do distract me," he said, and he pulled her close. "More than I care to think about." His mouth covered hers in a hungry kiss. This was not the fatherly peck on the forehead he had bestowed at the hospital. This was not the gentle good-bye kiss he gave her last night. This kiss was full of passion, one that seemed to be causing some weakness in Wendy's limbs. She clung to Eric's broad shoulders as the kiss deepened.

It took several seconds of pelting rain to bring her back to sanity. Pushing away from him, she couldn't meet his eyes. She was grateful, this once, for the incessant coastal rainfall. Starting the day with a cold shower wasn't pleasant, but it was effective, and she needed all the help she could get to save her from Eric. And, if she were honest, from herself.

"We'd better get out of the rain," he said softly, holding her for a moment longer. "Come on." They ran all the way to the police station, bursting, breathless, through the front door.

A bell rang as they entered, but the man behind the desk didn't look up.

Eric read the nameplate on the counter while he caught his breath and shook the rain from his jacket. "Corporal Standish?"

"Hmm?" The overweight man in a white undershirt was hunched over a desk reading. He peered over the top of the newspaper at Eric. "Well, now, speak up, son. What do you want so early in the morning?"

"My name is Eric Tremaine, and I wish to report a missing person."

With obvious reluctance, the weight-challenged corporal laid aside his paper and heaved his bulk to its feet. Judging from the double chin and overhanging gut, this was a posture he adopted only when necessary. As he came over to them, his glance fell on Wendy. "Oh, I didn't see you there, Wendy," he said, his attitude changing instantly, dramatically. He threw back his shoulders and tried to suck in his stomach. "My little girl still asks for you. You did wonders for her when she had the croup this winter." His stomach gradually dropped back into place. Taking another look at Eric, he said, "What can I do for you, Mr. . . . ? What's your name again, young fella?"

Eric looked at Wendy as if to say, *See? I was right to bring you.* She made a face at him.

"My name is Eric Tremaine, and I'm here to report a missing person."

"Humph!" The corporal took out an incongruous, Sherlock Holmes type pipe and began stuffing it with tobacco. "Who's missing?" He lit the pipe and puffed fiercely to get it going. The aromatic tobacco conjuring up a tweed jacket and country squire contrasted sharply with Corporal Standish, an overweight man in a sleeveless white undershirt.

From a back room, a younger, smartly uniformed officer appeared. "Hey, Ganzer!" Standish shouted over his shoulder. "Roust that partner of yours, and get over to Willy's place. They had another party last night. Left quite a mess and a lot of complaints."

Wendy watched John Ganzer casually help himself to coffee. She had to admit, he looked very handsome in the uniform. But from his cold nod, no one would have guessed they had ever met.

"You mean liquor and fights?" he asked, giving Wendy and Eric a subtle but thorough inspection. His clinical and impersonal scrutiny made Wendy feel about two inches tall.

"Dope too. Where is LeBoeuf, anyway?"

"Keep your shirt on, Corporal. We'll get right on it," Constable Ganzer said with an air of total unconcern. He sauntered off through another door.

"Humph! They sure don't teach manners and respect at the Academy anymore," the corporal commented. Wendy agreed. John Ganzer had acted more like the man in charge than the corporal.

"Well, what is it, Tremaine?" Corporal Standish asked, relighting his pipe. "Oh, yes, something about a missing person. Go on."

His patience clearly fraying, Eric tried once more. "I came to Shadow Ridge several days ago with my ranching partner. He's been missing since last night. I have a feeling he's in trouble."

"Missing-person reports can't be filed before forty-eight hours," the corporal told him. "Come back tomorrow."

Eric leaned across the counter, close to the fat face. "I know my friend is in trouble, Corporal Standish. Are you going to do your job or not?"

Red spots appeared on the corporal's cheeks. "You listen here, Tremaine," he sputtered. "I can't help you with your friend unless you bring me proof, not just your 'feelings.' When you do that, I will do what's necessary. In the meantime, we are up to our eyeballs in work here, and I have only two constables, both lazy. Your friend probably just found himself a comely lady at the hotel bar and spent the night elsewhere."

Wendy thought she would have to physically restrain Eric from launching himself at the corporal's throat, although how she would have managed that, she had no idea. His fists curled and uncurled in helpless frustration.

During the last volatile moments, John Ganzer returned,

followed by his partner, Claude LeBoeuf, the handsome-and-he-knew-it junior constable, wearing blue jeans and a white T-shirt. His tousled black hair told Wendy that he had not had time to do much more than dress. To her surprise, he called out, "Hi, Wendy," and winked at her. She had no idea he even knew her name. But why wouldn't he? As the most sought-after bachelor in town, he probably knew the stats on every female in town. He could have his pick.

Eric spared a scowl for the flirtatious lawman but quickly turned his attention back to the man at the desk. "You've certainly been no help at all, Corporal Standish," he said, his voice quavering with restrained fury.

"Humph!" Standish replied, and he returned to his paper.

Outside the office, Wendy took a deep breath of fresh air. The rain had stopped as quickly as it had come, but it looked as if more was on the way. "Where are you going now?" she asked Eric, shivering in the chilly morning air.

"To tell you the truth, I don't know," he said slowly. "I welcome all suggestions at this point." Wendy's experienced eye took in the dark circles around his eyes, probably due to lack of sleep. If she wasn't mistaken, he was bordering on a relapse.

"Have you eaten today?"

He shook his head.

"And I suppose you didn't sleep a wink all night."

He smiled, and her heart twisted at his sheepish grin. "Are you going to make me stand in the corner?" he teased.

"Pardon me for being concerned about your health and welfare," she snapped.

"It must be tough carrying around that huge chip on your shoulder," Eric said. He took her hand and tucked it under his elbow. His gaze told her he remembered the kisses they had shared. "Let's call a truce for today, okay? You're right. We need to eat. Where's a good place to get breakfast around here?"

She did her best to ignore the fluttering sensations his touch caused. "The Raven Motel has a decent coffee shop, but the best food is at Meg's Café."

"Meg's Café it is," he said, squeezing her hand. "Lead on, Ms. Hunt. I am completely at your mercy."

"That's a step in the right direction, anyway."

He laughed. Her spirits soared.

The café was empty. Wendy led them to a small table near the window, and they sat down. They had a good view of the misty bay, surrounded by tree-covered hills.

"It certainly is beautiful up here," Eric commented. "You have mountains behind you and the sea in front."

"I never get tired of the scenery, I must admit."

A middle-aged, friendly-faced Meg appeared to take their order. "What'll it be, folks? Say, Wendy, I haven't seen you in a dog's age. Not since you used to come in with Scott."

Wendy merely smiled. "We'll both have your Workman's Breakfast, Meg," she ordered. She closed the menu and handed it back to Meg. "And a pot of coffee." The waitress took the menu and left.

Eric leaned closer to Wendy. His eyes were dancing. "Thank you for saving me the trouble of deciding what to eat."

"You're welcome. I know it gives you a headache to think."

Eric chuckled. "I appreciate the way you anticipate my needs."

His intent gaze made her nervous. Turning away, she studied the whitecaps in the bay. "Looks like more rain is coming."

Eric agreed. "I sure hope that wherever Horace is, he's warm and dry."

"We'll find him. Don't worry," Wendy said quietly.

"I appreciate your encouragement," Eric said, absently pushing the salt and pepper shakers around. "I only hope we're not too late."

Meg arrived with a large pot of coffee and two heaping plates. The smell of bacon made Wendy's stomach growl. She turned pink.

"We're in total agreement there, Wendy," Eric laughed. "My stomach is about to turn vicious. You were absolutely right to

make us eat." Until some inroads had been made in their breakfast, neither one spoke.

"So, you and Scott came here often together, did you?" Eric
said finally. "I gather you two spent a lot of time together, from
Quentin's comments yesterday. Did you have any idea that
Scott might be in some kind of trouble?"

She shook her head sadly. "None," she whispered. "We
used to walk on the beach for hours, talking. I thought I knew
everything about him, but I see I didn't have a clue."

"Are you in love with him?" he asked, searching her face as
if the answer was of the utmost importance.

Wendy sighed. "You keep harping on that. Why don't you
just let it go? I told you about small-town gossip. People are
constantly imagining romance where none exists. I met Scott at
the hospital. He had sustained a laceration needing sutures—he
got a cut."

Eric grinned. "Thanks for the translation."

Wendy's lips spread into a reluctant smile. "Think nothing
of it. Anyway, Scott and I did spend a fair bit of time together.
I hadn't gone out much for almost a year, not since I'd left
Vancouver to come up here." She debated whether to tell Eric
about Richard.

"Go on," he said, looking intensely interested in what she
had to say.

This is why everybody loves him, she thought. *He makes
them all feel important, and who doesn't love someone like
that?* "If you must know, I left behind a disastrous relationship in Vancouver. Scott won me over because he was so easy
to be with, demanding nothing more from me than my friendship."

"You considered yourselves . . . good friends?"

Wendy nodded.

Eric was silent for a minute. Then he said, "You must have
wondered why he left town so suddenly without letting you
know. Maybe you felt angry, let down, disappointed?"

"Very astute of you. Yes, I did," she admitted. "Only, all the time, he was in trouble. I wasn't much of a friend to so easily believe the worst about him."

He reached out to cover her hand. "You had no way of knowing something had happened to him."

Meg returned and refilled their cups. Wendy was glad of the diversion. Eric was getting under her skin. She wanted to dislike him, but he was so darn sensitive and understanding just when she least expected it. But this morning's kiss had been a big mistake. They had kissed with a great deal of enthusiasm. With passion. Would he think she was simply an amusing diversion while he was in Shadow Ridge? His Northern belle? She was certainly going to have to reinforce her defenses, but how? The more time she spent with him, the harder it was to dislike him.

"Well, this breakfast ought to give us enough strength to find Horace," Eric said, scooping up the last of his eggs with toast.

"Yer lookin' for Horace?" Meg asked.

Eric looked up at her sharply. "Yes. Have you seen him?"

"Not since last night. Came in for supper. Nice old fella, though he kept to hisself. Just sat there in the corner porin' over some old maps. Tol' me he wuz looking for the sawmill."

Eric had the look of someone trying hard to remember something.

"What is it?" asked Wendy.

He leaned forward eagerly. "When I was in the hospital, I vaguely remember Horace talking to me about a sawmill. I just can't recall what he said about it. Is there one around here?"

She thought for a minute. "Yes. There's an old abandoned mill north of town. I'm pretty sure I could find it." She glanced at the lowering sky. "But looks like heavy rain soon."

"Then there's no time to waste." He threw some bills down onto the table and grabbed her hand. "Let's go."

Ten minutes later, they had found the logging road leading to the sawmill. He and Wendy bounced around in the pickup truck like clothes in a dryer.

"Sorry," Eric apologized as she practically bumped her

head on the roof. "I should have gotten new shocks before I came here." He reached out to steady her.

"Stop! There it is!" she shouted. Eric hit the brakes. She pitched forward and would have hit the dashboard hard if his arm had not shot out to prevent it. She clung to it like a limpet.

"Are you okay?" He looked pale.

"A little jarred but nothing broken." Her heart was beating unevenly, not entirely from the sudden stop.

"It looks like we can't go any farther in the truck. We'll have to walk," he said.

Jumping down from the truck, Wendy was sorry she hadn't worn her new gum boots. The road was muddy from the early-morning shower and very slick. When she stumbled, Eric's hand closed around hers, imprisoning it. She appreciated its strength. Picking their way carefully up a narrow path, they climbed steadily toward a decrepit old wooden building. Built on a hill, the sawmill could only be approached by a rotting wooden staircase, which crossed a narrow but steep ravine.

At the steps, Wendy let go of Eric's hand and started up. "Be careful, for heaven's sake," Eric cautioned, but it was too late. The second step was rotten, and as soon as Wendy put her weight on it, she fell right through. She slid all the way down the ravine.

"Wendy, are you all right? Answer me!"

She was vaguely aware of the intense concern in his voice, but she was having trouble breathing. She tried to call up to him, but nothing came out when she opened her mouth.

Eric slid right into her at the bottom. With utmost gentleness, as if she were a priceless possession, he cradled her in his arms. "Please say something, Wendy. Are you all right?"

She nodded, and managed to whisper, "I'm fine. Just got the wind knocked out of me." He rocked her gently, patting and rubbing her arms. She concentrated on taking deep breaths. It took her a few moments to realize he had become very still, and when she looked up at him, he was staring at the tangled brush near them. Following his gaze, Wendy saw it too—the red-checkered pattern of a lumberjack shirt. She sat upright.

Her movement brought Eric to life. "I think we've found Horace!" he exclaimed, and he scrambled toward the bit of red color.

Then the rain began.

Chapter Six

He's alive, Eric!" Wendy shouted when she reached the older man. "He has a pulse." She tried to hide her own misgivings. Horace was suffering from exposure, and she noticed caked blood on his scalp.

Eric managed to squeeze in closer.

"It looks like he hit his head on something," she told him. "He's lost a lot of blood."

"Can we get him up to my truck?"

The naked fear on Eric's face tugged at Wendy's heart. "No, don't move him. He might have a neck or back injury. Do you have a cell phone on you?" He shook his head. "Then you'll have to drive back to the clinic, get the ambulance here."

"That'll take too long."

"If he has a broken neck and we move him, it could cause permanent paralysis. He's been here overnight. Another twenty minutes isn't going to make much difference."

Eric made his decision without much deliberation. "You're right. I'll go."

Wendy peeled off her jacket and laid it over Horace. Eric tore

71

off his own coat and handed it to her without a word. "Thanks," she said, tucking the coat around Horace's frail-looking body. "Now, go, and be careful."

"I'll be as quick as I can," he promised, and then he scrambled up the hill. Wendy heard a few choice words on his way up.

When the truck had left, the gloom seemed to close in on Wendy. "Hang in there, Horace. Help is on the way," she whispered close to his ear. It made her feel better just to hear her own voice.

Without moving him, Wendy tried to assess what other injuries Horace might have sustained. She carefully probed his arms and legs, but nothing felt grossly out of place. She touched Horace's hand. It was frigid. It was also curled around something. Gently, she pried it open and discovered a black rock. It looked like the same Haida argillite Quentin had shown them. What would it be doing here, clutched in Horace's hand? Had Horace discovered something about the stolen argillite? She slipped it into the nearest pocket on the jacket covering Horace and made a mental note to tell Eric when he returned.

Wendy started shivering. Her drenched cotton sweatshirt was no match for the bone-chilling cold. She couldn't get close enough to Horace to share whatever heat they had between them. All she could do was keep the coats snugly around him and shelter him from the rain with her body. Her teeth were chattering so loudly, she hoped Horace might wake up and tell her to be quiet. He didn't.

An eternity passed before she heard a vehicle coming up the bumpy road. *The ambulance!* Voices above her were asking where the patient was, and Eric's louder one was shouting orders impatiently.

"Wendy! Where are you? Call out, so we can locate you."

"I'm here! You're right above me. Bring down a neck brace and a back board."

Eric wasted no time in his descent. The hill was even more slippery now, and he slid right into Wendy, unable to control the last part of his descent. He handed her the white neck brace he had tucked inside his shirt.

With shaking fingers that were aching from the cold, Wendy slowly slipped it into place around Horace's neck. "I feel better moving him with that on," she said, her words slightly slurred from her shivering. Eric stared at her. She felt suddenly, absurdly self-conscious. "I must look a sight," she said, halfheartedly lifting an arm to push her wet hair out of her face. "Who came with you?"

"Dr. Chandler and Janet. And you look beautiful to me," he told her with a softness in his tone that brought tears to her eyes. Eric yelled up to the others. "Okay up there! Let the board down. Easy does it." The back board, attached to ropes, was slowly lowered to them, and Eric and Wendy pulled Horace out from under the brush as carefully as they could.

They gently rolled him onto the hard stretcher. Eric wrapped two woollen blankets around his friend and strapped him snugly to the board. "All right!" he yelled. "Start the winch!"

He glanced at Wendy and gave her hand an encouraging squeeze. "You look half frozen yourself. I can hear your teeth chattering." Wendy felt his warmth and wanted to bury her face in his solid chest. Instead, she gritted her teeth tightly and murmured, "You're so g-g-good for a girl's ego."

A couple of times the stretcher threatened to swing wildly out of control, but Eric managed to straighten it out. Once it was up, he hollered, "How about helping us up now?" The winch spooled out rope, and Eric tied it around himself, picked up Wendy, and hollered. Within seconds they were at the top of the ravine, back on solid ground.

Joe and Eric quickly hoisted Horace into the ambulance and jumped in beside him. Janet took the wheel, and Wendy climbed into the passenger side. "You clearly need a keeper, Wendy," she said without apology. "What on earth happened? Here, wrap yourself up in this blanket."

Gratefully, Wendy snuggled into the blanket, smiling wanly at Janet's no-nonsense manner. "As soon as my t-t-teeth are under c-c-control, Janet, I'll tell you. It's a long story." She was still shivering when they turned into the hospital driveway.

Eric and Joe brought in the stretcher. Janet looked at Wendy and said, "You can't do any more right now for Horace. Go and get yourself out of those wet clothes before you catch pneumonia. And for goodness' sake, do something about your hair."

"If I didn't see the worry in your face, I might think you were heartless, Janet. That is worry, isn't it?"

"Darn right it is, kiddo. Now, scram. Nurse's orders."

Wendy knew Janet was right. A hot shower was what she needed. She tried to run up the hill to the dorm, but her movements were slow, as if she were slogging through mud. Likewise, when she tried to remove her clothes, her fingers felt stiff. Finally, she stepped into the shower. The heat surrounded her, penetrating her cold joints until she could move normally. As she dressed, something niggled at her, but her thoughts still seemed scattered, even if her body was functioning again. If her brief exposure to the elements had done this to her, she could only imagine what it had done to Horace. She hoped they had found him in time.

By the time she returned, Dr. Thomas, Joe Chandler, and Eric were huddled in discussion outside Horace's room.

"He's suffered a blow to the head as well as hypothermia," Dr. Thomas was saying. "I won't beat around the bush, Tremaine. Your man needs to get to Vancouver as soon as possible. I've already called a neurosurgeon there, and I contacted the airport. They can have a Cessna ready to transport him in thirty minutes." Dr Thomas checked his watch. "That will get you into Vancouver well before dark, weather permitting."

"You anticipated my consent, Dr. Thomas," Eric said wryly.

"I would have overridden your objection anyhow, Tremaine. Legally you're no more responsible for this man than I am."

The two men seemed to take each other's measure. "Glad we're in agreement, then," Eric said.

Dr. Thomas commandeered Wendy to accompany their

patient to the Vancouver General Hospital. The fact that she was off for the next three days made her the logical choice. There was just enough time for her and Eric to pack overnight bags and head to the airstrip. At the airport, Eric's pallor concerned Wendy almost as much as this enforced trip to Vancouver. She hadn't wanted to return to the scene of her heartbreak quite so soon.

"How are you feeling, Eric? You look terrible," she said bluntly. "I mean, you were pretty sick yourself, and not that long ago."

"Horace came here to help me," Eric whispered raggedly, ignoring her question. "He's in this predicament because of me." He turned to face her, and she saw the raw emotion on his face. "It should be me lying there, not Horace."

The small plane had been in the air less than ninety minutes when it began its descent. By the time they landed, it was 3:30 in the afternoon. The pilot had radioed ahead to have an ambulance waiting, and as soon as the plane door opened, Horace's stretcher was efficiently transferred to the vehicle. Eric insisted on staying with Horace in the back. The paramedic directed Wendy to the front seat. The sirens and flashing lights of their vehicle moved city traffic out of their way, cutting the time to the hospital in half. Pulling into the Emergency bay, the paramedic parked, exited the vehicle, and went around to open the back doors. He and the other attendant took Horace on his stretcher and disappeared from view.

As soon as she entered Vancouver General, Wendy felt its familiarity enfold her. This was where she had trained and where she had worked after graduation. She knew every nook and cranny of the place; she knew its heartbeat. This was where she had met Richard. This was where she had returned his ring. She caught sight of the paramedics heading toward a bank of elevators.

"Where did they take him?" Eric asked, looking around frantically.

Wendy grabbed his arm. "This way," she said, and they managed to catch up to the attendants as they pushed Horace's stretcher down another corridor. "Where are you supposed to take him?" she asked the nearest paramedic.

"Neuroradiology," he told her.

Wendy realized that Horace had remained unconscious since they found him at the sawmill. Not a good sign, but for Eric's sake, she tried to keep her feelings from showing. At their destination, the paramedics pushed Horace past a reception desk and directly into a large room with a big table and a large scanning device.

As the minutes ticked by, Eric began pacing. He was about to say something when an Asian man in his thirties, dressed in green scrubs, entered the room. "I'm Dr. Keith Cheung," he announced. "Are you the folks from Shadow Ridge?"

Eric stepped forward. "Yes, we are. I'm Eric Tremaine, and this is Horace Duvall. And Miss Hunt is the nurse who came with us."

"Is Horace a relation, Mr. Tremaine?" the doctor asked, looking at the chart.

"No," Eric said, "but close enough. As far as I know, he has no family."

"From what Dr. Thomas told me, it sounds like bleeding under the skull. We'll run a CT scan now to verify the diagnosis, and he'll likely need surgery immediately."

"Isn't brain surgery risky?"

"It is never without serious risk, but if this is a subdural bleed, I can assure you, the need for immediate intervention outweighs any risks."

Eric looked grim. "So you're telling me he *might* die with surgery but he *will* die without it?"

"I'm afraid I am." Dr. Cheung held Eric's glare without flinching.

Two attendants came in and effortlessly, it seemed, slid Horace onto the scanning table.

"They're going to do the scan right now," Dr. Cheung explained. "As soon as I see it, I'll be back to speak to you. Please take a seat in the waiting area so I can find you." Dr. Cheung followed them out of the room and turned in the opposite direction.

"Do you know anything about this doctor, Wendy? Is he competent?" Eric paced back and forth, shaking his head. "Does he look like a brain surgeon to you?"

"He has an excellent reputation," Wendy said soothingly. She led Eric to the waiting room Dr. Cheung had mentioned. There, she spotted a vending machine and, digging into her purse, found enough change to buy two coffees. Eric stood at a window overlooking the parking lot, deep in thought. He accepted the cup she handed him and automatically took a sip. She saw the worry lines etched into his face and wished she had something encouraging to say.

When Dr. Cheung found them, he told them the CT scan had revealed a large blood clot in the temporal lobe of the brain. He explained the procedure he planned, as well as the risks, and asked Eric to sign the consent form. Eric looked as if he had been blindsided with a sledgehammer, but he signed the paper.

"Wendy! Is that you?" said a male voice from behind them. She recognized that voice, would know it anywhere. Memories flooded her mind at the sound.

She swung around and faced him. "Richard."

For months after she left Vancouver, she had dreamed of meeting him again. She had rehearsed dialogues they would have, searching for the exact phrasing, the exquisite nuances, that would shake him to the core, would make him realize what he had lost. Now her mind failed her; she could do nothing but stare mutely at the man who had broken her heart a year ago.

Eric coughed. Stepping forward, hand extended, he said, "I'm Eric Tremaine, a friend of Wendy's." He smiled stiffly. "You must be Richard."

"So, Wendy told you about me?" Richard said it with a

touch of smugness, which complemented the immaculate white lab coat covering an expensive three-piece suit.

"Not exactly," Eric said blandly. "I heard her say your name just now."

Richard seemed taken aback. He gave Eric a closer scrutiny. "I see." He frowned. Turning to Wendy, he smiled in that way that used to turn her to mush. She was surprised that it didn't. "Are you back here at VGH again?" he asked.

Shaking her head, she said, "No, Richard. I came with a patient. With Eric." She felt her cheeks grow hot. "He's not the patient. I mean, Eric and I came with his friend, who is the patient." She caught a look from Eric and closed her mouth. It was hard to think straight with Richard standing there. "I heard about your promotion to chief of ophthalmology."

His eyebrows rose. "Even way out in the boonies? I'm surprised." His look said, *Aha, so you still care about me.* "How long will you be in town? Can we get together for dinner or something?"

Wendy wanted to say, *Why would we get together for anything, Richard?* but she couldn't get the words out. She just muttered helplessly, "We're . . . maybe, uh . . . could . . ."

"We were just thinking about getting a bite to eat while my friend goes into surgery," Eric said, filling in the conversation gap Wendy had left. "Would you like to join us?"

Richard checked his watch. "You know, I'd really like to catch up, but I've just been called for a consult in the ER. Where are you staying, Wendy? How long will you be in town?"

She had not even thought about those two questions, which was very unlike her. "To tell the truth, I have no idea. I didn't plan that far ahead."

Richard's eyebrows went higher. "Wendy Hunt, not planning every minute? That is curious. Is it the northern air or . . ." He looked from Wendy to Eric, and his eyes narrowed. "Something else?"

Eric put an arm across Wendy's shoulders. His touch seemed to bring her out of her fugue state.

"How's Cindy?" she asked. *Just to let you know I haven't forgotten.*

"Fine, as far as I know." Richard said without enthusiasm. "Look, I'd love to stay and chat, but I've gotta run." He backed up. As he turned to go, he said, "Listen, if you're staying in town for a while, please look me up. At least you know where I'll be." He waved. "Nice to meet you, Truman," he added before he disappeared around the corner.

Wendy stood rooted to the spot long after Richard was gone. She doubted he had an ER call. More likely, Cindy was waiting for him. It seemed so long ago that she had once yearned to be the woman waiting for him.

"Are you okay?" Eric asked her, gently shaking her shoulders.

She nodded slowly. "Yes, I am," she said, and she realized she was. Ever since she had walked into the hospital, she had been subconsciously expecting to run into Richard. Now it had happened, and Richard was the same, but his charm had lost something. She had watched him walk away without feeling that her life was over. Not only had she survived the test but, except for a moment or two of awkwardness, had passed with flying colors. Eric had stepped up just in time. Despite her concern for Eric and Horace, her heart felt lighter than it had for a long time. "Not only am I all right, I'm starving."

Eric glanced at a clock on the wall. "Five o'clock, already. No wonder we're hungry. Dr. Cheung said we'll have quite a wait." He feigned obeisance to her. "In this foreign place, O mighty hunter, I look to you to lead us to food. And while we're at it, we have to think about where we will spend the night. Any ideas?"

"I see you already have the hang of getting on my good side, *Mr. Truman.*" She giggled. "There's food on the second floor, if I remember right."

The cafeteria was filling up with staff on supper breaks. It took several minutes to get through the line with their trays. Spying a table for two, Wendy threaded her way to it, followed closely by Eric. Transferring her plates from the tray to the table, she said, "You know, I never even thought about where we'd stay while we're here," she said to Eric. "I might still have relatives in the city, except . . ." She stopped.

"Except what?"

She stuck her teabag into a pot of steaming water and jiggled it up and down. "It's just that we really haven't spoken for years. Aunt Lily is my father's sister."

"Why the long silence?"

"Family squabbles. My father left us when I was ten, and Mother broke off all contact with his family," Wendy told him with all the emotion of a weather report. She took the teabag out of the water and set it down on a spoon. "I remember visits to their house with my parents, but that was so long ago," she said wistfully.

"It sounds like you miss them." Wendy shrugged but said nothing. Eric bit into his roll. "You know, you're a grown-up now, Wendy. Why not call your relatives if you want to see them?"

"You think I could just call out of the blue? It has to be almost fifteen years since I last saw them."

"What's the worst that can happen? They hang up on you. Then we try Plan B, whatever that is," he said matter-of-factly.

She thought back to her childhood visits. Her aunt and uncle's wonderful old house overlooked a marina crammed with boats of all shapes and sizes. Having no children of their own, they had lavished time and attention on Wendy, who in turn had soaked up every drop of affection. She could not remember hearing one argument between her aunt and uncle. Unlike her own troubled home, theirs was filled with love and harmony. Now, Eric had set her thinking. Perhaps Aunt Lily and Uncle Mark had missed her too. Would they be interested in seeing her after so many years?

"First, I'll have to find out if they still live here. But you're right. I should call them, if only to thank them for being so kind to a lonely little girl. And if they invite us to stay, I'll accept."

"Good for you. But count me out. I need to be here tonight. With Horace."

"I guarantee you won't get any sleep in the hospital," she said, not sure why she was pressing the issue.

He shook his head firmly. "I appreciate your concern for me, but I'd rather stay here. I'll sleep, trust me."

"Whatever," Wendy said, leaving it at that.

The supper crowd was thinning. Wendy couldn't help but notice a statuesque brunet walk over to a table on the other side of the room. Behind her, with his hand lightly touching her back, was Richard Farnsworth. They sat down opposite each other, and Richard leaned in close to his companion. It was an intimate pose. And the woman, Wendy noted with raised eyebrows, was not Cindy. Richard had moved beyond both of them. For the first time, Wendy saw what life with Richard would have been like.

"Penny for your thoughts," Eric said, touching her hand lightly.

"Oh, sorry," she said, and she turned back to him. "Nothing, really. Just people-watching."

Eric followed her glance. "Isn't that Richard, the doctor we just met?"

She nodded and took a bite of her sandwich. She hoped Eric would not pursue the subject.

"When we first saw him today your reaction—temporary brain freeze—made me wonder if he was your disastrous relationship."

What was wrong with the man? Her no-trespassing sign should be flashing bright red by now. Could he not read plain English? "Richard and I were engaged. We broke up. That's it."

Eric waited expectantly.

With a sigh of exasperation, Wendy added quickly, "He decided he preferred my roommate, Cindy. I gave him back his ring."

"I'm sorry," Eric said gently. Reaching across the table, he laid a hand over hers.

Wendy felt a tingle all the way up her arm and quickly withdrew her hand. But as she stared at Richard and his brunet across the room, she was surprised to realize that, for the first time, it didn't hurt. She had loved Richard—then. Now she could watch him flirt with a beautiful woman, and her pulse remained steady.

"Another penny," Eric said again gently.

"My mother always said that men won't buy the cow if they can get the milk for free," she mused aloud.

Eric smiled. "I believe I've heard that saying. And Richard wanted free milk."

She felt warmth creep up her face.

Eric was no longer smiling. "My guess is that he didn't get any from you, so he turned to Cindy."

Studying her hands intently, Wendy nodded.

"Taking your mother's advice saved you a lot of grief, Wendy."

"I know." She met his eyes. "But I always hoped that some-one would love me enough to—" She broke off, embarrassed.

"Buy the cow first?" he said with a crooked grin. "Tell me about your father."

"My father? Why?" The question startled her.

"Because I hear that girls marry their fathers—figuratively speaking, that is. You know, they fall for what they saw in their fathers." He paused. "Oh, now, there it is," he said.

"What?"

"Your shop-closed look. I've seen it before." His tone was cajoling, not accusing.

"If you really care so much," she said, "I'll tell you every-thing I know about my father. He broke all his promises. I haven't seen or heard from him since I was ten."

He was silent for several moments. Then he asked, "Did your mom ever remarry?"

"Of course not," Wendy said with force. "She never got over my father. Still hasn't. He broke her heart."

Eric's left eyebrow rose a notch. "And yours too, I suspect." He held her gaze until she dropped her eyes.

Wendy felt an ache in her heart area, a literal ache, as if something wanted to escape, to break free. Once again, Eric leaned close and covered her hand with his warmth. As if his touch had transfused truth serum, Wendy could not resist confessing, "I missed him so much at first, I cried myself to sleep every night." She withdrew her hand, breaking the contact. Holding his steady gaze, she said, "Then I got over it. I grew up. Mom and I did just fine without him."

"Right, I can see that," Eric muttered. "That explains so much." He leaned back. "Well, not to change your favorite subject, but I've been thinking about Scott," he said casually.

"Was that a crack?" she asked.

He smiled.

"I was being a bit sarcastic because getting you to talk about your real feelings is like eating Jell-O with chopsticks."

"What doesn't kill you makes you stronger," she retorted, smiling.

"Anyhow, I'd like to visit the magazine editor who sent him up to Shadow Ridge. I'd appreciate your knowledge of the city to get me there, if you want to accompany me."

She nodded. "I'd be happy to be your guide."

"I've been thinking of something else too. Remember when we talked about Scott's being taken away for medical care?" She nodded again. "Is it possible we could find out if he was brought here?"

"All we need is access to their records." She lowered her voice. "Can you hack into a computer?" She laughed at that but grew excited as another thought struck her. "If he was brought here four weeks ago with serious injuries, it's possible he might still be here. And that information we can find out."

"Scott sure is a lucky guy," Eric said with a sigh. "Your whole attitude changes when you talk about him. You two sure are good . . . 'friends.' "

Wendy sighed. "For Pete's sake, will you please stop harping on that? I'm beginning to think Scott ran away from Rosewood because you bored him to death by repeating yourself."

"Very funny. Let's check the records." Eric looked annoyed, and Wendy wondered if she had hit a nerve.

The admitting office was closed, and the only fact they could determine from Information was that Scott Ellerslie was not currently an inpatient. "He could be a security code," Wendy suggested. "If a patient needs to remain anonymous, he's listed as Smith on all public sites. Only staff working on the unit would know the real name."

"Another dead end," muttered Eric.

Horace was still in the OR when they returned to Neurosurgery. Wendy asked the nurse in charge if Eric could spend the night in the lounge. Eric's recent hospitalization and convalescent condition gained him so much sympathy that the nurse offered him the on-call doctor's room.

"You really should tone down your smile a little," Wendy told Eric coldly. "The poor woman looks like she's about to swoon."

Eric raised his eyebrows in surprise. "Well, you made me sound like a half-dead corpse just looking for a place to expire." He gave her an exaggerated grin and then waited for her reaction. Her expression didn't change. "See? It doesn't work with you. And I have this sucker turned up full force."

She couldn't keep a smile from spreading across her face, but she turned away. He didn't need encouragement in the charm department. He had it in spades, and she was not as immune to it as she pretended. "I'm going to the lobby to make a phone call," she told him, leaving him with his smitten nurse, another casualty of the Eric Tremaine smiling machine.

Chapter Seven

Wendy found a pay phone in the hospital lobby and thumbed through the White Pages, looking for her aunt's number. For one panic-filled moment, she couldn't remember Aunt Lily's last name—Adamson, that was it. The Adamson list went on for half a column, but fortunately Wendy recognized the address. She dialed before she lost her nerve.

"Hello?" A cheery voice answered on the second ring.

"Hello," Wendy said. "Is this Lily Adamson?" Her heart vibrated in her chest. What if Aunt Lily hung up on her?

"Yes. Can I help you?" she asked.

As Wendy recognized the warmth and vitality of her aunt's voice, she felt ten years old again. "This is Wendy Hunt," she said. "Steven Hunt's daughter." Wendy waited to hear Aunt Lily's response. She would take her cue from that.

"Oh, my goodness gracious!" Lily's reaction was immediate and spontaneous. "Steven's little girl, of course." Aunt Lily laughed and cried at the same time. "You sound all grown-up. Where are you calling from? Is it really you?"

Wendy teared up at the welcome in her aunt's voice. "I'm

here in the city for the weekend. I wondered if I could drop by to see you and Uncle Mark."

Lily didn't hesitate. "Of course, Wendy darling. You're always welcome here. And I insist that you stay with us. I have hoped for so long to hear from you." Her aunt's voice caught on the last word.

Wendy was overwhelmed by how much those few words meant to her. They soothed an ache she had not known existed. Wiping away a stray tear, she said, "I . . ." She cleared her throat and began again. "I'm glad to hear your voice too, Aunt Lily." After a short pause, she said, "I'm at Vancouver General at the moment—"

"Is everything all right, dear? Are you sick?" Lily cut in.

"No, no, nothing like that," Wendy hastened to say. "I came with a friend—I'll tell you all about it when I see you. It's a long story."

They spoke for another few minutes, and then Lily offered to send Mark to pick her up.

"I couldn't let you put him out at this hour," Wendy protested. "If you don't mind, I'll get a taxi to your place. I'm . . . not sure how long I need to be here. Would eight-thirty or nine be too late?"

"Good heavens, no, child. It'll give me time to bake some brownies and tidy up a bit. Bye for now, Wendy dear." She hung up.

Wendy smiled. After so many years, she was about to see her aunt and uncle again. If anyone had told her that morning that she would be here right now, she would have thought they were touched in the head.

The elevator doors opened. As Eric walked toward her with his blazing smile, her heart literally skipped a beat. Until now, she had always thought the expression "weak in the knees" was nothing more than a cliché, but she was fast becoming a poster child for romantic clichés. *I seem to be as susceptible to the Tremaine mystique as everyone else*, she thought. *Not good, not good at all.*

"Well, Horace is out of surgery and holding his own, they say, so that's good news," Eric said, a worried frown appearing on his brow. Then he asked, "What does 'holding his own' mean in medical terms, anyway?" He seemed so fretful that Wendy could not help touching his arm to express her comfort. Their gazes met, and a spark sprang between them. Taking her hand, he pulled her slowly into his arms. "Something like this?" he whispered against her hair.

Though she tried to resist, Wendy couldn't stop her arms from circling his waist. Resting her head against his chest, she gave herself up to her feelings. It had begun to dawn on her that she and Eric would soon be parting ways—forever. She would return to Shadow Ridge; Eric would go back to his ranch with Horace. Their first meeting had set her early-warning system on high alert with good reason. This man had slipped past her defenses right into her heart without firing a shot. But he was going to leave her just like the other men she had loved and lost.

Reluctantly but firmly, she pulled away from him. Looking anywhere but at him, she said, "I don't think that's what it means." Her voice didn't sound like her own.

Eric, looking exhausted, rubbed his eyes as if his head ached. "Did you manage to find your relatives?" he asked.

Wendy recounted her phone conversation with Aunt Lily, and as she did so, the tension between them eased. "I thought I would wait with you a bit before I went to Aunt Lily's, just to see how Horace is doing—if you'd like." As she made the offer, she wondered whether it was the wisest course of action. She just couldn't bring herself to leave him so alone.

He looked relieved at her offer, like a man brought back from the brink. "Why don't we grab another coffee and make some plans to retrace Scott's movements while he was in the city?" he suggested.

In her head, Wendy heard her mother's voice say, *Daughter, don't be a fool. Run as far and as fast as you can while you still can.* She ignored it. "Sounds like a plan," she told Eric.

During the next hour, Wendy tried to imprint on her memory every moment of her time with him. They made plans for him to pick her up at her aunt's house in the morning and visit Scott's magazine editor to see where that led. Before they parted, she gave him her aunt and uncle's address and phone number, not entirely convinced he would turn up.

At eight-thirty, Eric walked her to her taxi. "See you tomorrow. I promise."

In her experience, a promise didn't mean very much, but she found herself praying all the way to her Aunt Lily's that this one would be kept.

As Eric watched Wendy's taxi disappear into the dark Vancouver night, he felt more alone than he could remember. He was in a foreign country with his best friend struggling to live, his brother missing, and the woman of his dreams slipping away.

Making his way back to the cafeteria, he bought another cup of coffee and sat at the same table he had shared with Wendy, just to feel close to her again. He was pathetic. When had he started falling for her? Was it the moment he had plucked her out of the ditch and held her, shivering, in his arms? Was it watching her take care of Phoebe Littlefeather, or Mr. Peters? Or was it when she had trusted him enough to let him dress her wounded foot? He had felt a response from her then, but he had ruined it, trying to keep focused on Scott.

That was a joke. With Wendy around, he had a hard time remembering he even had a brother. All he knew was that he was falling in love with her—wholly, completely, and quickly. He doubted Wendy would believe him for a second if he told her. She wouldn't dare admit that the spark between them was more than just physical attraction.

But that hurdle was insignificant compared to the other reason that Eric held back from declaring his feelings for her. He was convinced that Wendy and Scott were an item—or, at the very least, had been falling in love before he disappeared. She would not admit it, naturally, but he could not ignore the signs: her face glowed when she talked about him, and her gaze softened. When—Eric refused to think *if*—his brother was found, he and Wendy must be given a chance to explore their bond. Once before, Eric had come between Scott and a woman he cared for. That act had driven a wedge between the brothers that had, now, culminated in Scott's disappearance. Eric would not let his feelings for another woman interfere again. Even if it killed him.

It took Wendy thirty minutes to get from the hospital to the Adamson house but another five to work up enough courage to ring the bell. Without Eric beside her, she suddenly felt like half a team. When the porch light came on, she took a deep breath to steady her nerves. Footsteps and excited voices from within accelerated her heart. Then the door swung open, and it was too late to run. There stood Aunt Lily, exactly as Wendy remembered her, only not as tall.

"Wendy?" Aunt Lily looked her over with an expression Wendy couldn't interpret. "You've grown so much. And you've changed." She took a moment to study her niece and then added, "I see a lot of your father in you. I never noticed it when you were younger. Well, come in, come in." She pulled Wendy inside and gave her a hug that left them both breathless. "We have missed you so much!" her aunt exclaimed, echoing Wendy's thoughts. "You've become a lovely woman, just like I predicted. Didn't I always say she'd be a beauty, Mark?"

Her uncle stepped forward with a warm smile on his face. "You did, darling. You were correct as usual." He enveloped his niece in a gentle hug. When Uncle Mark released her, he said, "Yes, indeed, you are beautiful, Wendy."

She blushed. "Thank you," she murmured. "I really appreciate you having me—"

"Nonsense, you're family. It's been too long as it is since

we've seen each other," Mark said. "Let's not stand in the hall-way. Come inside, my dear, and give me your bag." He took it from her and disappeared upstairs with it.

Wendy followed Lily up a few steps to the spacious, vaulted-ceiling living room. After taking her coat, Aunt Lily immedi-ately showed Wendy her room, where her overnight case awaited her. Then, talking nonstop, Lily gave Wendy a fifty-cent tour of the rest of the house.

Wendy enjoyed seeing it again, but it made her realize there were gaps in her memory of it. She remembered the home fondly from her childhood, but everything looked different from an adult perspective. Regret for all the missing years with her aunt and uncle washed over her.

Wendy remembered what her mother had told her as a child. *We will never set foot in that woman's house again. She poisoned your father against me.* Wendy found it diffi-cult to believe that the woman who had just welcomed her with open arms could have been that hurtful, conniving, and devious.

Lily brought Wendy back to the kitchen, where Mark had prepared a pot of tea. "There you are," he said when they re-turned. "Tea's made."

"Can you tell we've redecorated a bit since you came here as a child?" Lily asked, quickly filling a plate with delicious-looking brownies. She poured tea into three cups. "Milk or sugar?"

"Just milk, thanks," Wendy said. "I do remember your brownies, Aunt Lily. Daddy and I always snuck some after supper—" Without warning, she started crying. Silent, tears-running-down-the-cheeks crying.

Aunt Lily simply took her niece into her ample arms and held on. Wendy couldn't understand why she was crying, but she couldn't stop the flow. Eventually the cloudburst was over, reduced to a few hiccups and sniffles, and Wendy pulled away from her aunt. "I'm so embarrassed," she murmured. "I have no idea why I'm being such a baby." She took a tissue from the box Uncle Mark surreptitiously moved over to her, and she blew her nose.

"Memories can do that to me too, dear," Aunt Lily said gently. "And I suspect being here has unleashed memories of happier times for you. Times spent with both your parents. Don't you ever get to see your father?"

Wendy shook her head. "As far as I know, he dropped off the face of the earth. I haven't seen or heard from him in twelve years."

"He lives in Kitimat now. He remarried, you know. A lovely girl from there."

Pain ripped through Wendy's heart like a scalpel through flesh. While her lonely mother had suffered all her adult life because of her husband's treachery, Steven Hunt had lived a pain-free existence. Had he ever spared a thought for his first family? "He already had a wife," Wendy said, every word steeped in disapproval.

"Oh, dear, I don't think you understand at all—"

"Lily, my darling," Mark interrupted. "It's getting late. Perhaps we should let Wendy get some rest for now. We have the weekend to catch up."

Wendy was grateful for Uncle Mark's intervention. She had for a moment forgotten that Lily was her father's sister. She was kind—naturally she would want to defend him—but he had broken his vows and destroyed his family. He was indefensible.

"Of course, Mark. How thoughtless of me. A good night's sleep is just what you need, isn't it?" The expression of pain and confusion on her aunt's face gave Wendy a pang of remorse.

"It has been a long day," Wendy said, wondering whether this visit had been such a brilliant idea, but politeness compelled her to put her best foot forward. "But I would like one brownie to eat with my tea if I may." She offered a conciliatory smile and was gratified to see her aunt respond in kind.

"You said you came down from Shadow Ridge," Lily said.

"I don't think I've ever heard of it. Is it up north? And what have you been doing there?"

"Lily, dear, you're asking Wendy too many questions. She can't give you a dozen years of history in the time it will take to eat a brownie." Mark turned to Wendy. "Just the highlights tonight, my dear. You and your aunt have all weekend to catch up."

Wendy liked her uncle. His soft brown eyes and easygoing manner soothed her raw nerves. "To answer your first question, Aunt Lily, Shadow Ridge is a fishing town about four or five hundred kilometers north of here. I've been working as a nurse at the hospital there for the past year."

"Oh, you're a nurse? How grand. Did you know she was a nurse, Mark? I didn't either. Where did you take your training?"

"I trained at Vancouver General a few years ago."

"You mean you were living in Vancouver all those years and never even phoned? What a shame." Uncle Mark didn't sound angry, only disappointed.

"Hush, Mark." Lily gave her husband a jab in the ribs.

"To be honest," Wendy explained, "I guess I felt that my father's family was not mine anymore." She shrugged. "I'm not sure exactly why I called you tonight. It just popped into my head."

"Well, I don't care why you called. We're glad you did. Family is all we have in the end. You are family—always have been, always will be. Are you married? Children?"

Wendy shook her head with a smile. "No to both questions, Aunt Lily. I was engaged a while back, but it didn't work out."

Mark couldn't suppress a yawn. "Ladies, I'm still a working man, and it's way past my bedtime. If you don't mind, I will leave you at this point. Good night, Wendy. I'll see you tomorrow sometime, and if my wife tries to keep you up all night, push her into the bedroom at the other end of the hall, and shut the door firmly behind her." Mark kissed his wife on the lips, and a tender look passed between them. The love between them was almost palpable.

"Good night, Uncle Mark. See you tomorrow," Wendy said, blushing as he kissed her on the forehead.

"Don't worry, darling. I'll let Wendy get to bed. Come, dear."

She followed her aunt upstairs.

"We have our own bathroom, dear, so this one is all yours. We always keep it stocked for guests. Here are some towels. Help yourself to whatever toiletries you need—soap, toothpaste, shampoo, whatever."

"Thank you, Aunt Lily. You're very kind." Wendy said it earnestly, knowing it was the truth.

Lily gave Wendy another fierce hug, and there were tears in her eyes as she pulled back. "It's been so long, my dear. We have so much to talk about." She kissed her cheek and went to her room, closing the door behind her.

Wendy's emotions were in chaos. She was with her father's sister, and somehow that was bringing together the past and the present. Memories crowded in—things she had managed to keep from intruding into her daily life. But always over-shadowing that life had been the hovering ghost of her father's betrayal. He had been unfaithful to his wife, and he had deserted his daughter, and those actions had left deep scars on both his victims.

As far as Wendy knew, her mother had never even looked at another man. She had raised Wendy on a meager salary, in a small trailer. Wendy had gone to school wearing clothes from the Salvation Army—perfectly usable, just old-fashioned and ill-fitting. In junior high, where sporting the latest fashion craze was terribly important, Wendy had always been one or two fads behind. She'd never quite fit in.

Not that she'd wanted to belong to one of those snooty cliques, but she would have given anything for a best friend. She'd never had a close enough girlfriend to share secrets or talk about boys, or do homework with. Her teachers acted as if they felt sorry for her, the cliques ridiculed her wardrobe, and the boys ignored her—the worst thing boys could do to a girl. The one time in high school when a boy walked her home from school, Wendy's mother came marching out of their run-down trailer and proceeded to interrogate him. He got out of there as fast as he could and never came near Wendy again. At first, Wendy was mortified by her mother's behavior. Later, overhearing the boy tell some friends that she and her mother were crazy, she couldn't argue with her mother's bitterness toward the male gender.

As she matured, Wendy's romantic soul had wanted to prove her mother wrong. When Richard Farnsworth swept her off her feet, Wendy believed that his love would repudiate her mother's theories. Yet, despite her desire to trust in that love, Wendy found herself wondering what Richard was doing every second they were apart. Was it a case of a self-fulfilling prophesy? No. Upon reflection, and having seen Richard again, Wendy realized that he was exactly the type of man her mother had told her he was. So where did Eric Tremaine fit into this conundrum?

Wendy splashed cold water onto her face, brushed her teeth, changed into her nightgown, and slipped under the scented sheets. Although she was afraid her whirling thoughts would keep her awake, exhaustion prevailed.

That night she dreamed—vivid, painfully realistic dreams. She saw herself as a little girl on a playground, and someone was pushing her on the swing—something her mother might have done on occasion. But then she became aware that the person pushing her on the swing was her father. Every now and then he would grab the swing and give her a loving hug before pushing her higher and higher as she delightedly commanded. It felt like a happy time.

As it was with dreams, the scenes changed rapidly and out of sequence. First she was seeing her father pick her up and toss her into the air. In another snippet they were eating popcorn at a movie. At some point she was in pajamas, and he was reading her a story before bed. In the dream, she felt her father's love, and her child's heart adored him.

Abruptly the scene changed to Deborah Hunt standing at the front door. As she cried bitter tears over the man driving away, a young Wendy stood next to her mother and watched, dry-eyed and silent, as her adored father left her behind. The child was sure her father had said, "I wouldn't be leaving now if you had been a good girl."

In the dream, Wendy covered her ears to protect herself from those hateful words. With a whimper, she sank to the ground, weeping uncontrollably.

Chapter Eight

Waking up, Wendy felt her last dream press down on her like a great weight. She lay in the soft bed and opened her eyes to sunshine spilling into her room and the smells of coffee and bacon. Although the dream had seemed real, it began to slip away from her mind almost immediately, the way shadows melt away from the light.

Presently, Aunt Lily's cheery laughter drifted upstairs, and Wendy pushed back the fluffy, patterned quilt and put her feet on the floor. Then came a tiny knock on the door. "Come in," she called.

Aunt Lily opened the door slightly and peeked in. "I hope I didn't wake you," she said, coming in a little farther when she saw that Wendy was up. "It's after nine o'clock," she added with an apologetic smile. "I thought you should know that someone named Eric Tremaine has come to call on you. A delightful young man." Aunt Lily closed the door as she left, but not before Wendy had caught the happy grin on her aunt's face.

Wendy dressed quickly, stopping in the bathroom only long

enough to attend to her most urgent needs. *He had come!* She rushed downstairs, slowing only when she entered the kitchen.

With a "Good morning, Aunt Lily" and a casual "Hi" in Eric's direction, she made a beeline to the coffee and poured some into a mug with a Stanley Park view on it. Eric appeared to be studying a city map laid out on the kitchen table. He looked up, and as their glances met, he smiled. Unaccountably, Wendy felt awkward. She looked away first. Before she could ask him about Horace, Aunt Lily came over to her and kissed her on the cheek. "How did you sleep, dear? Was the bed comfortable enough for you?"

"It was perfect, Aunt Lily. I was asleep as soon as my head hit the pillow." She decided not to mention the dreams that had troubled her. No doubt being in this house again had stirred up old memories and thoughts of her parents.

"What can I get you two for breakfast?" Aunt Lily asked, already pulling out bread, jam, eggs, and bacon. "Your Uncle Mark has already had breakfast and gone down to the marina to work on his boat. He does it every good weekend we have at this time of year."

"I don't need a thing, thanks, Mrs. Adamson," Eric said, without much conviction.

"Nonsense. You young people don't know how to take care of yourselves properly, rushing off without the most important meal of the day. I simply won't allow it. Eric, how do you like your eggs? And don't tell me anything about cholesterol, because I don't believe a word of it. Eggs have been around a lot longer than cholesterol. Wendy, what about you?"

Eric didn't hesitate. "Scrambled," he said. "Thanks." Wendy agreed.

Soon, aromas of bacon, toast, and coffee again permeated the cozy house. With Lily engaged in her cooking, Wendy turned to Eric and asked him about Horace.

"He's off the critical list," Eric said with a grin. "In fact, he woke up early this morning."

"Thank God," she breathed. "What's his prognosis?"

"Dr. Cheung said he should be just fine," he reported, still beaming.

"Does he remember what happened?" She didn't want to come right out and ask, *Was he pushed, and does he know who did it if he was?*

He shook his head. "He can't remember exactly how he got to the bottom of the ravine. He recalls going to the sawmill, but the rest is a blank. As far as I'm concerned, the farther away he is when he remembers, the better. Dr. Cheung said it would be safe for him to leave tomorrow."

"You mean you're leaving?" Wendy blurted out. She was mortified it had sounded so pathetically desperate. "I mean, of course you should. It's just that Scott—" *Get a grip, girl,* her mother would have said. Wendy silently concurred.

Nervously she started clearing their dishes. "If you have to go back to Rosewood, I can still try to find Scott—ask questions when I go back—"

Eric grabbed his plate from her hand. "Whoa, I haven't finished yet, Wendy. What's the rush?" He set his plate down again. "I said Horace can leave. He should get back to the ranch to recuperate. I'm not going anywhere. And I certainly don't want you to go around by yourself asking questions back in Shadow Ridge."

He didn't add, *Look what happened to Horace.* He didn't need to. She gave him a brittle smile. "It's okay with me if you have to go—"

"So you've said—twice now." He held up two fingers.

"You'll need to leave sooner or later. . . ."

"That's three." He held up three fingers.

"I just thought . . ." She didn't know what she thought. What on earth was wrong with her today? Even her aunt looked puzzled. Wendy averted her eyes from Eric's searching gaze.

"I made arrangements for Horace and booked us a morning flight to Shadow Ridge tomorrow. Like it or not, I'm going back with you."

"Well, if you're sure . . ." At his look, she fell silent.

"Eric was telling me about your recent adventures, Wendy," Aunt Lily said, apparently unaware of the cross currents between her two guests. "He tells me you plan to do a bit of detective work to track down his absent brother. It all sounds very mysterious. And a little dangerous."

"Well, so far we've run into a few dead ends, Aunt Lily, but there is a lead Eric wants to follow while we're here." Leaving Eric's plate on the table, Wendy cleared away the rest of the dishes and began washing up. Behind her, Aunt Lily drew Eric's life story out like saltwater taffy. He told tales of his horse ranch in Rosewood, mentioning Horace over and over. It drove home to Wendy how much the older man meant to Eric. Clearly, Horace was family.

Before long, Eric turned the tables. He had Lily sharing stories from her own childhood. To hear her tell it, the two Hunt children were feared and loved far and wide for their famous practical jokes and loyalty to friends. More telling even than the stories she related was the love in her voice. It was obvious that Lily adored her brother.

Standing at the kitchen sink washing dishes, it struck Wendy that she could not recall a single time that her mother had ever spoken kindly about or to Steven Hunt. For the first time in her adult life, Wendy was seeing her father through loving eyes.

A tear splashed down into the sink in front of her. She had to leave the room before the floodgates opened. She dried her hands and turned away. "I've got to get ready," she managed to say, then ran upstairs.

In the bathroom, Wendy splashed cold water onto her face as more tears poured down her cheeks. Sadness overwhelmed her. She was incapable of stemming the flow. For several minutes, she fought for control. Coming to her aunt's home had been a terrible idea. She should have gotten a hotel room last night and then returned to Shadow Ridge today. Eric could follow leads in Vancouver by himself. All he needed was a map and a taxi.

An image of Scott's laughing face rose up in her mind, and she directed her thoughts toward him. She and Scott had been kindred spirits. They had found laughter in the midst of their separate bitter regrets. She had told him about Richard's betrayal; he had poured his heart out to her about Eric's control issues. Their common hurt bound them quickly. She credited Scott with getting her past the worst of Richard's betrayal. Thanks to Scott, she began to believe she might trust love again, if it came.

Remembering Scott renewed her desire to find him, to discover what had happened to him. She blew her nose and squared her shoulders. Carefully, she combed her hair. After applying more makeup than usual, she was pleased to see only a trace of telltale redness in her eyes. "Thank you, Scott," she whispered as she checked her reflection once more. "I'll do my best to find you."

If they had noticed her lengthy absence, Eric and Aunt Lily made no mention of it when she reappeared. Two heads were bent over the map on the kitchen table, with Aunt Lily giving Eric confusing directions to an address in downtown Vancouver. Wendy smiled at them just as Eric looked up. His intense stare made her uncomfortable.

Aunt Lily rose to her feet. "You look lovely, Wendy dear," she said, looking from one guest to the other.

"Thanks, Aunt Lily." Wendy reached over and hugged her. Aunt Lily returned the embrace with genuine affection. Wendy cleared her throat and turned to Eric. "Where do you think we should start?" She had made up her mind upstairs to keep things on a professional level; they were partners with a common goal—to find Scott.

In the same neutral tone he said, "We're going to see the magazine editor who sent Scott to Shadow Ridge for the native-art story. He may be able to help us track Scott's footsteps here in Vancouver. Your aunt was just giving me directions to the place." Eric sounded dubious.

"So I heard," she said, breaking into a grin. "You don't go into town much, do you, Aunt Lily?"

"I must confess that your uncle always drives." She shrugged apologetically.

"Not to worry, Aunt Lily," Wendy assured her. "I lived here for years. I know my way around." She glanced at the address Eric had written on a piece of paper on the table. "I know where this is, but it'll cost us a fortune to take a taxi there. Are you game for a bus ride?" she asked him.

"Sure. You're the boss." He saluted.

"Keep that in mind, mister, and we won't have any trouble."

"Just be sure to let me know if you need a big, strong man to protect you, so I can do my small part in the scheme of things, ma'am." Eric winked at Aunt Lily and followed Wendy out.

As soon as they were away from the house, Eric took Wendy's arm and stopped her. "Is everything okay? I noticed you'd been crying when you came downstairs." He looked worried.

She couldn't avoid the question, so she gave him the short answer. "I'm just a little emotional today. I think it's being here after so many years. Also, I dreamed about my parents last night."

"One of those dreams that feels absolutely real?"

"Yes, exactly."

"Care to talk about it?"

"I can't remember the details, only that it seemed very sad. As you so astutely guessed, I've had a good cry, and I feel better now." She started walking again, and he joined her. "But if I overreact to things, please just ignore me, okay?"

"I might not be able to tell, but I'll try," he said, grinning. "I envy women being able to get things out of their system with a good cry. It's so much more polite than beating someone to a pulp. Or spitting," he added with a twinkle in his eye.

They had to run the final steps to catch their downtown bus.

Indian Art Magazine was located in a seedy neighborhood. As it turned out, even that was too generous a description for the urban mess of overgrown shrubbery and broken sidewalks they had to negotiate. In the Yellow Pages, the location was advertised as *close to Granville and Broadway*. In reality, the magazine was several blocks and a park away from Granville Street. Eric and Wendy nearly walked past it.

"There it is!" exclaimed Wendy, pointing to a window. The sign was barely visible against the backdrop of a nearly opaque, cracked window. Except for the magazine's sign, the peeling gray clapboard building was exactly like all the others on the block.

Eric squinted through the dirty window. "This must be it." He looked around the neighborhood, his expression grim. "How on earth did Scott find this place?"

"Not very inspiring, is it?" Wendy remarked, walking up the three cement stairs to the door. "I wonder if this venture is still viable."

"I was just wondering that same thing myself," Eric remarked, following her up. He looked for a bell to ring. There was none. "Well, let's see if there's anyone here." He turned the knob, and the door opened. Cautiously, he entered first, positioning Wendy behind him. "I'll be the big, strong man now," he whispered. She didn't argue.

As they opened the door wider, a bell tinkled, announcing their arrival. Eric and Wendy ventured farther inside. Their footsteps echoed on hardwood floors dull from lack of care. The musty, dimly lit room was bare of furniture.

"Do you suppose they've gone fishing?" Wendy said, not a little unnerved by the hollow sound of her voice in the empty room.

Before Eric could answer, an inner door opened, and a man came out. "You're late," he said briskly. "You were supposed to be here an hour ago." He looked as if he had dressed in a hurry—his shirt was half tucked in, his hideous tie at half-mast—and he needed a shave. *And a shower,* thought Wendy, catching a whiff from behind Eric.

"Are you Gordon Holloway?" Eric asked, stepping closer.

"Yeah, that's me. What took you so long?" he repeated, peering intently at Eric. Abruptly, he straightened and stepped back. "You're not the buyer. Who are you?"

Eric took a step backward as well. "Obviously you were expecting someone else. I came here to ask you about my brother, Scott Ellerslie."

"Scott who?" Holloway ran an unsteady hand through his already messy hair and turned away. "I mighta known they wouldn't show. Who wants to buy a rotten, stinking corpse of a magazine?"

Wendy and Eric exchanged glances. "Mr. Holloway, we came from Shadow Ridge, where you sent Scott Ellerslie on assignment some time ago," Wendy said, following Holloway back to his office, a tiny cubicle with a desk piled high with magazines, a couple of filing cabinets, and a wooden swivel chair behind the desk.

Holloway stopped and turned to her. "Ellerslie . . . Shadow Ridge . . ." He scratched his head.

"You hired Scott to write an article for your magazine, *Indian Art,* remember?" Eric prodded.

Gordon Holloway stared at Eric for several moments. "Have we met?" he asked.

"No, I'm sure we haven't," Eric assured him dryly. "But we're here to find out if you have seen or heard from Scott Ellerslie since you sent him to Shadow Ridge."

The man shook his head. "Nope. I remember him now. Spoiled kid but desperate to work, he said. Never did turn in an article. Doesn't matter anymore. The magazine is flat broke. Couldn't have paid him anyway." Holloway plopped down in the swivel chair and rested his hands on the desk. "Anything else?"

Eric took a deep breath. "It may be that the reason you never got an article from Scott was because he had a serious accident in Shadow Ridge."

A spark of interest leaped into Holloway's eyes. "Really?

"I'm sure it would have made great copy for your art magazine, Mr. Holloway," Wendy said coldly. "If it were still up and running, that is. But, frankly, we're here to see if we can retrace Scott's steps after he left you back in January."

Holloway took his time looking Wendy over before answering. Unconsciously, she folded her arms across her chest, where his eyes seemed fixed. Eric followed Holloway's glance and stepped in front of Wendy to block the man's view.

"Well?" Eric said, breaking Holloway's concentration.

The editor pushed some papers around on the desk. "That was a long time ago. I may have sent the boy to check out Indian art exhibits. In fact, there's a big display near Stanley Park once a week, like a farmer's market, only it's native art. All the area artists bring or send their pieces there to be sold." Holloway pointed to a calendar on the wall. "It's on Saturdays from ten to six."

"That's today." Eric checked the time. "It's almost noon. Can you get us there, Wendy?"

"Piece of cake," she said, smiling. She was beginning to feel useful.

"Mr. Holloway, I am sorry about the demise of your magazine, but I'm more concerned about what happened to my brother. Would you like me to let you know what I find out?" he added dryly.

"Sure thing, let me know. I hope he's okay. Good kid, just a little . . ." Eric glared at him. "Never mind."

Eric grabbed Wendy by the elbow and ushered her out of the office.

"Good luck," Holloway called as they left the building. Retracing their steps to Granville, they caught a bus marked STANLEY PARK, which dropped them off at the entrance twenty minutes later.

"Wow, it sure is busy around here," Eric remarked as he was jostled from behind. "It also looks like it's going to rain. Do you think they'll pack up the art exhibit if it does?"

Wendy laughed. "If rain stopped everybody in Vancouver, we'd never get anything done. You must get a lot of rain in Seattle as well." She craned her neck to see over the crowds of tourists heading toward the park. "Look," she said pointing to an open area to their left. "I think that's it over there."

They headed in the direction of the exhibit, Wendy practically running to keep up with Eric's long strides. "Could you slow down a bit, please?" she puffed. "They're not going to close up shop in the next five minutes."

"Sorry." He stopped abruptly, and she bumped into his broad back. "Wendy, do you see that character over by that exhibit? He's wearing a bright yellow scarf, and it looks very much as if he's arguing with the vendor."

Wendy followed the line of his gaze. "Sure. Wow. That scarf adds life to his otherwise grubby trench coat. I gather you don't think he's just doing some intense haggling over the price."

"If I'm not mistaken, that is Claude LeBoeuf, your ladies' man Mountie."

Chapter Nine

Wendy stared for several seconds, and whether the man felt her eyes watching him or was simply checking out the crowd, he turned and looked straight at her. As soon as his glance met Wendy's, he shook his head at the vendor and hurried away.

"I think you're right, Eric," she said with a puzzled frown. "I wonder what he's doing here in Vancouver. And he's dressed in civvies . . ."

"And that colorful neckwear," Eric said with a grin. "Let's go check out that exhibit and see what, if anything, we can find out."

They made their way to the vendor who had been talking to LeBoeuf. The merchant stood in front of his table of native treasures: various totem poles, some wooden, others black and shiny, plus an assortment of handmade silver bracelets, pendants, and rings. On a second table he had laid out neat rows of beaded moccasins trimmed with fur. He even had a few paintings set up on easels for sale, and he watched over his domain like a rooster guarding the henhouse.

Eric picked up a black totem like the one Quentin Whitefoot had carved. Checking the price, he whistled. "This little baby is selling for two hundred bucks." He held it in his hand, as if judging its weight. "I don't think this is the argillite Quentin uses. It's not heavy enough. This feels like plastic." He turned it over in his hand. A tiny sticker on the bottom read GENUINE SLATE.

"Do you want it?" asked the proprietor, taking it out of Eric's hands and putting it down on the table. "Can't you read the sign?" He pointed to a poster forbidding customers to handle the merchandise. "Two hundred dollars, if you want it."

"That seems pretty expensive for four inches of plastic," Eric said, hoping he sounded like a tourist looking for a bargain. Wendy had crept in right beside him after perusing the jewelry.

"This is genuine argillite, straight from Slate Mountain," the man said. "See?" He showed him the sticker on the bottom.

"Why is that so expensive?"

"Very rare rock. Difficult to get. Hard to carve. You want it?" He held it up but retained possession of it.

Eric shook his head. "Real argillite is heavier than this. I think this is a fake."

The startled look of fear that flashed into the native's eyes told Eric that the man knew very well he was selling phony totems. "You don't want it, go," the proprietor said abruptly. He pulled a tarp from under the table and began covering his collections. "I'm closed."

No way would they get any leads on Scott from this shyster. Eric took Wendy's hand and led her away from there as quickly as he could. "That man knew he was selling fakes. And he was afraid when I challenged him." Wendy looked as if she had thought of something. "What?"

"I just remembered that after we found Horace at the sawmill, I noticed he was clinging to a small piece of what looked and felt like argillite." She dug into her jacket pockets. "Darn! I've got a big hole in this pocket. Wouldn't you know? I must have lost it. But I'm sure it was the real thing. Do you suppose that the stolen argillite was being stored at the sawmill?" she asked excitedly.

"It's possible. That would explain why both Scott and Horace had 'accidents.' They both got too curious. . . ."

His voice trailed off as he gazed at her. Wendy had been falling for his brother before he'd come on the scene. No matter how Eric felt about her, he had to remember that. He stared at her for much too long. Why did she have to be so appealing? "Wendy?"

"Yes?"

"I wish you wouldn't look at me like that." With immense effort, he put more space between them. "We're partners, strictly business, and I will remember that."

"By all means, stay focused," she murmured.

If only she knew how hard it was to do that with her walking beside him.

All at once, someone pushed Wendy from behind, knocking her off balance. Before either of them could react, the assailant snatched her purse and took off running. Eric gave chase and within seconds had disappeared into the crowd, leaving Wendy stunned and alone.

Rain began to fall in earnest while she was wondering what to do. Had Eric caught the thief? Or was Eric lying somewhere, bleeding and beaten? Her imagination immediately conjured several gory scenarios so frightening that when Eric came out of the crowd, running toward her, she flung her arms about his neck and held on. "Eric! You're okay!"

"Are you all right?" he asked breathlessly when they pulled apart slightly. He ran his hands up and down her arms and torso, automatically checking for injuries. The look of concern in his eyes would have pleased her if she hadn't been so worried about him.

She punched him in the chest. "I'm fine. What were you doing, running after a mugger that way? He might have had a weapon. You could have been killed, for goodness' sake. Then where would I be? With no purse and no protector and—"

Eric pulled her close and kissed her—hard. When he drew back, she was calm again. "I appreciate your concern for me," he said, chuckling. "It's very touching, but I'm afraid I couldn't get your purse back. Sorry."

"You kissed me." It was an accusation.

"Sorry. I thought you were verging on hysteria. It was either going to be a kiss or a slap. I made a judgment call."

"Good call, I guess," Wendy said. Put that way, it wasn't a big deal.

"It's really starting to pour," he said, wasting no more time analyzing the kiss. "We have to get inside somewhere. There's a restaurant. I'm starving anyway."

He grabbed her hand again and pulled her along behind him. Since a lot of people had the same idea of seeking shelter from the rain, they arrived to a waiting crowd of hungry patrons.

"It's a thirty-minute wait," the hostess informed them, as they shook the rain off their jackets. "We have lots of room in the bar, if you want to wait there. Your name will be paged when a table is ready."

"I need the ladies' room," Wendy said, pointing helplessly to her wet hair and clothes. She went in and checked for rain damage. The good news was that she had worn a light Windbreaker that had protected her top half, and her bottom half was not that wet. Her slacks would be dry by the time they finished lunch. Her hair was the bad news. Although she kept it short, the wind and rain had combined to make a bird's nest out of it. Normally she would pull a comb out of her purse, but she had no purse. She tried smoothing down the worst of it with her hands, but it popped up as soon as she let go. The mirror must have been a man's invention, she thought, feeling miserable.

At length, having decided she couldn't stay forever in the restroom, she opened the door. Eric emerged from the men's room, and they met in the hallway. He held out his comb. "I just realized that without your purse, you haven't got your . . .

uh, essentials. All I have is a comb, but you're welcome to borrow it. It's clean."

"You've redeemed your gender for inventing the mirror," she said, and vanished quickly back into the ladies' room. As she worked at the tangles, she had to give Eric points for anticipating her needs. Due, no doubt, to vast experience with women. That thought dampened her appreciation of the comb.

Her hand stopped in midair as a thought occurred to her. Her purse had contained more than lipstick and a comb. It held a photograph of her father. A precious, irreplaceable picture. After her father had left for good, her mother had systematically destroyed every trace of him, even cutting him out of family pictures. As a child who sorely missed her father, Wendy had rescued one solitary photograph of him. In her teens, she hated not having a father. It had left a deep void, but for her mother's sake, she never mentioned him. Yet deep in her heart lay a yearning she could barely admit to herself. She wanted him back in her life. Despite his betrayal, despite her angry feelings about him, she had carried his picture with her always, keeping it safe, desperately hoping that he would somehow come back to her.

From time to time she took the photo out to study. She would wonder where her father was, whether he thought about her life: her growing up, going to school, her first date, first prom, getting married. Often she imagined how they would meet. He would tell her how much he loved her, how much he had missed her, and then he would say how sorry he was for leaving her when she had needed him to stay.

Although she never would have admitted it, she had wanted her father to walk her down the aisle when she and Richard married, but she'd had no idea where to find him. Now she did know, thanks to Aunt Lily, but now she had no fiancé, so it didn't matter anymore.

The sadness pressed in on her again. *Not now,* she groaned inwardly. Splashing her face with cold water, she blinked rapidly, refusing to cry again. She pushed away the futile dreams. Dreams didn't come true. She knew that now. But Scott needed her to find him. Eric was waiting for her in the bar. Life went on.

Scrunching her short hair as stylishly as possible, she left the restroom. Eric was now seated at a booth with a view of the rain-slicked street. She had been in the washroom long enough for a table to open up.

Silently, she handed him back his comb. He took it, placed it in his jacket pocket, and looked her over. "You look mahvelous, dahling, simply mahvelous," he joked with an exaggerated accent.

Wendy laughed appreciatively, thankful for Eric's sense of humor, and sat down across from him.

A waiter came to the table, and they both ordered coffee. After he had gone, Eric leaned forward. "Do you suppose that mugging had anything to do with our visit to that particular exhibit?"

"That's what crossed my mind," Wendy said. Her heart started thumping as she thought about the experience. "In all my years of city living, I was never mugged before."

"Something to tell your grandchildren, *eh?*" He exaggerated the *eh* to tease her about the Canadian locution.

Just then, a man approached their table. "I believe this is yours, miss," said Claude LeBoeuf, dropping Wendy's purse in front of her. She shot a glance at him. Sure enough, under the grubby attire lurked the Mountie. An angry scowl marred his handsome looks. Peeking out from under his tattered coat was a yellow scarf, an ensemble that Wendy felt confident was not RCMP issue.

Eric moved over and motioned the constable to sit. Glancing furtively around, looking more like a criminal than an officer of the law, LeBoeuf slid in beside Eric.

"I chased down the mugger and recovered your purse," he told Wendy in such a low voice that she had to lean forward to hear him. "I took a chance that you might have come here to get out of the rain."

Wendy quickly checked her wallet. Her father's picture was still there.

"Money's gone, I'm afraid. Credit cards too. I hope you've phoned in a report of them being stolen." The Mountie's businesslike manner was completely at odds with his shabby appearance.

"I was only carrying a few dollars and no credit cards."

LeBoeuf made no attempt to hide his surprise. "Not one?"

"I never wanted to get into debt. Is that a crime?"

He shook his head. "Hard to believe but not a crime. All I can say is, you'll make some man very happy, not racking up the debts. I know. My ex-wife put me in a big hole using one of those things."

Wendy couldn't decide which surprise was greater: LeBoeuf's personal remark about her or that he had an ex-wife. She glanced at Eric. He looked surprised too.

"What are you doing here, and in that getup?" Eric asked LeBoeuf.

"Not expecting to run into you two, that's for sure. And I would appreciate it if you forgot you ever saw me here, got it?"

"No, we don't 'got' it," Eric said, his voice rising with annoyance. "Did Wendy's purse-snatching have anything to do with the man we saw you talking to? He sells fake argillite totems, by the way."

LeBoeuf gave Eric a sharp look and said, "Quiet, man. I'm risking my neck to talk to you at all. Just listen. I'm only gonna say this once. I'm working undercover. I was assigned to Shadow Ridge to find out about possible corruption, including smuggling of expensive art objects out of the country. You people could've blown a cover I spent weeks setting up here. The guy you talked to didn't like your attitude, so he sent one of his goons to mug you two. Thought he'd give you a scare, so you'd get out of his face. I spotted him and followed. He won't be bothering you anymore."

The chill in his voice kept Wendy from asking for details.

"You're an undercover agent?" Eric said.

LeBoeuf rolled his eyes. "Say it a little louder, Tremaine. That guy across the street didn't hear you. Look, I gotta scram." He started to leave, but Wendy put her hand on his arm. He sat back down. "What?"

"What happened to Scott? How does he fit into this?"

LeBoeuf couldn't hide his reaction in time. For just a moment he looked like a trapped animal before the hard mask dropped over his face again. She had touched a nerve.

"Ellerslie poked around too much. He wouldn't shut his mouth, and it got him killed, probably." Leboeuf sounded petulant.

"You think he's dead?" Eric asked bluntly.

"I told you to keep your voices down. I don't know if he's dead. I don't know any more than you. Doc Chandler told us that Quentin Whitefoot dragged him to a remote beach the night Ellerslie disappeared. I went out myself. Nothing. My guess is that whoever sent Ellerslie over that cliff finished him off and dumped him at sea. We'll probably never find his body."

Wendy glanced at Eric, but his face gave nothing away. "Or he could still be very much alive."

"If it makes you feel better to think that, go ahead. My guess is that he started asking too many questions, got too close. That's not smart in a small town where people want to keep secrets."

"Is that a threat, LeBoeuf?"

"It's just good advice. And here's more—don't crowd my investigation."

"And Horace? Did he get too close too?" Eric asked, his voice icy.

"He found the smugglers' hiding place at the sawmill, didn't he?" Wendy added, happy to wipe the smirk off Claude's face.

"Horace is lucky to be alive," said LeBoeuf. "I, for one, would be very interested to hear what he has to say about his so-called accident at the old sawmill."

"He doesn't remember anything about it," Eric said quickly.

LeBoeuf looked as if he were weighing the truth of that

statement. He shrugged. "Sounds like you two are getting in over your heads too. If you want my advice, you will go back to Washington, Tremaine, and you, Wendy, should think about a transfer out of Shadow Ridge." At Wendy's expression, he added, "Not a threat, just more good advice."

Eric and Wendy's waiter hovered nearby, waiting to take their order. LeBoeuf pulled his coat together and started to leave. "Just so you know, I never saw you two, and I was never here, got it?" LeBoeuf slid out of the booth and quickly walked out of the restaurant.

Eric and Wendy stared at each other. "Can you believe that guy?" Eric said, his mouth curving into a smile.

Wendy giggled. "He sounds like a villain out of *Dirty Harry*."

After the Mountie had left, the waiter moved in to take their order. Looking at his name tag, Eric said, "Sorry, Mike. We haven't had a chance to look at the menus yet. Could you give us a few minutes?" Mike put his notepad back into his pocket and went to another table.

"What do you think?" Wendy asked as she watched Eric's face. "Did you believe all that undercover stuff?"

"Let's just say I'm not convinced our French lieutenant is entirely trustworthy. However, he did say one thing I happen to agree with."

"What's that?"

"I think it would be wise for you to consider leaving Shadow Ridge at your earliest convenience."

"I just can't up and leave without notice. Besides, I'd have to find another job, another place to live."

"You're a nurse, for Pete's sake. You can find a job anywhere. I'll even give you a job myself, if I have to. Just give your notice, and pack your bags."

"And just what kind of a job could you give me? Shoeing horses?"

"Please don't argue with me, Wendy. You are not to endanger yourself anymore for Scott, and that's the end of it."

The command was unmistakable.

"I see why Scott called you tyrannical," she muttered. Eric frowned.

The rain had tapered to a fine drizzle. Glistening streets were again filling with people eager to resume their interrupted activities.

"Would you *please* leave Shadow Ridge?"

She shook her head. "I can't. Not right now. I promised to help you find Scott, and I don't renege on a promise. Besides, we're partners, and that means working side by side, as equals. What one can't do, the other does. We have each other's back and—"

"You could be describing identical twins, not partners," Eric said dryly.

"You're not responsible for me, Eric."

Eric whistled softly. "Wow. Déjà vu," he said under his breath.

"What do you mean?"

"It's just that you sounded exactly like Scott. That's something he would have said. In fact, he probably did more than once," Eric told her, half smiling.

Mike reappeared to take their order and offered no comment when each ordered the classic hamburger, fries, and cole slaw. Eric added, "And keep the coffee coming." Mike picked up the menus and disappeared into the kitchen.

Wendy glanced at Eric, who was staring out the window. Was he thinking about Scott?

"We'll find him, you know. He's going to be okay."

"From your lips to God's ears," he said grimly. "You seem to have a lot of faith in my brother."

She nodded slowly, not sure where this was going. "He may be your little brother, Eric, but he's got a good head on his shoulders. He'd want you to trust in him."

"You're right. It's hard to stop seeing him as my kid brother. I've looked out for him all my life. You make me consider a guy I don't even know," Eric said slowly. His eyes held hers.

"I guess I've let him down. You were right, Wendy. I drove him away, and what happened to him is my fault."

She smiled gently. "Scott told me about the gold-digging fiancée you paid off and sent packing. He was angry that you were right, as much as anything. His pride was hurt. He'd picked the wrong woman, and you fixed things for him again," she said. "In the past you may have been overbearing, dictatorial, smothering—"

"Okay, okay, you've made your point."

"You didn't let me finish. What I'm trying to say is, you can't blame yourself for Scott's disappearance from Shadow Ridge. He had to find his own way sooner or later. I'm expecting, when you see each other again—and you will, I just know it—you and he will be able to patch things up. Your relationship will heal, and everything will turn out . . ."

"Happily ever after?" Eric's eyebrows shot up. "So there's a Pollyanna buried under that cynical shell?" He regarded her thoughtfully. "Your own story isn't finished yet either, Wendy. Maybe you'll be able to make peace with your father someday too."

"I'm afraid that's all very ancient history, Eric." She took a deep breath, and as she exhaled, she tamped down the sting of emotion his comment had aroused in her. He had an unsettling way of sailing blithely into treacherous waters. "Anyway, this hour is reserved for your family neuroses and our continued partnership in finding Scott."

He smiled. "Since you're just stubborn enough to continue sleuthing about alone, I will accept your terms . . . partner," he said lightly.

She couldn't help the laughter that bubbled up in response to his good-natured banter. She reached out to seal the deal with a handshake, unable to ignore the tingle that ignited in her at his touch.

"What's our next move?"

"Our next move?" Eric's face was unreadable. He stared out the window, apparently giving her glib question some thought.

The silence lengthened.

"Anytime you'd care to share your deep thoughts, partner . . . ," Wendy prompted him. "This is not the time to be the strong, silent type."

Mike brought their hamburgers and a carafe of coffee. As soon as he left, Eric spoke. "First, I think we should see Quentin Whitefoot again. He may know something about why an art vendor in Stanley Park is selling fake totems marked genuine. I'd also like to visit the place where Scott fell and talk to Dr. Joe Chandler. Maybe he knows something."

Wendy nodded. "Good ideas all. In fact, I was thinking those very things." He raised his eyebrows. "I was," she said defensively. "You see, already we think alike. This should prove to be a profitable partnership," she declared, as matter-of-fact and businesslike as fit the occasion.

They both proceeded to make short work of lunch.

Chapter Ten

The rain had stopped by the time Eric and Wendy finished their late lunch, but even as they paid the bill and collected their jackets, the somber sky threatened to open up once more.

Stepping out of the restaurant, Wendy sniffed the cool air. "Don't you love the smell of the ocean after a rain? I think I'll always want to live by the sea," she mused, checking her watch automatically. "Oh, my goodness, it's already four o'clock. Where has the time gone? I have to leave tomorrow." She used the singular personal pronoun deliberately. He didn't need to think she was counting on his coming back with her.

Eric smiled down at her as if he knew exactly what she was thinking. Glancing at the lowering clouds, he said, "I doubt we're going to find that vendor again, although I have a few questions I'd like to ask him. And since the hospital search for Scott came up empty, I have no other leads to follow." He took her by the arm. "I've heard about your famous Stanley Park, and here we are. I'd like to see it with you before we go back." The very slight emphasis he put on *we* could have been Wendy's imagination.

Wendy selected a tour book Eric could take home with him as a souvenir, and together they walked through the zoo. When they reached the aquarium, Wendy kept up a steady stream of informative chatter. "This isn't as big as Sea World, by any means," she told him with her tour-guide intonation, "but it is the best in Canada. A lot of American tourists come here." She watched Eric's face as he studied the white Beluga whales cavorting in their outdoor pool. Was it possible he hadn't seen one before? When he spoke, she realized his thoughts had been on a different track.

"It's fascinating to me that whales mate for life," he remarked.

Where did that come from? she wondered. "I beg your pardon?"

"I bet you wish men could be as faithful as whales, don't you?" His look challenged her, dared her to be honest.

"You would win that bet, Eric." How different her life would have been had her father stayed. "I saw what being left did to my mother. How could he just . . . go?"

"I don't know." He leaned against the aquarium rail, studying the whales.

"Anyway, as I told you before, it's ancient history." She knew it was a lie. Her eyes filled. She turned away from the whale pool, surreptitiously wiping away a stray tear.

Eric followed her. "Somehow I don't think you believe that any more than I do."

Wendy turned to face him. "I accepted a long time ago that I can't change the past. And I admit that I'm a little emotional today. Seeing Aunt Lily again has stirred up memories. But I *am* over it—believe me. After my father left, life went on. I grew up, became a nurse, and I have a very full life. I'm just fine."

"I wonder," Eric said, clearly not convinced.

"Don't bother your head about it," she told him brusquely, feeling like a boxer against the ropes. "But perhaps you'd care to tell me how many women *you've* loved and left?"

The minute the words escaped her lips, Wendy wished she could call them back. She had no desire to hear Eric's romantic history. Wanting to escape his probing gaze, she walked quickly toward the exit. He caught up to her near the gift shop and grabbed her arm. "Do you really want to know the answer to that question?" he asked in a low voice.

She whipped around and came face-to-face with his intense blue eyes. Threads of desire skittered along her nerves; his nearness melted away all thought, leaving only a deep yearning. His eyes seemed to probe deeply into her heart.

"I don't think you're ready yet," he whispered raggedly, letting her go.

Seconds of tension-filled silence ticked by. "I think it's time to go back to Aunt Lily's," Wendy said finally, torn between hope and fear. Hope that Eric could never betray the woman he loved, and fear that he was exactly like her father. She shivered. "It's going to rain again. Maybe we should take a cab."

By the time their taxi pulled up in front of the Adamson house, the off-and-on drizzle of the day had become a downpour. Demonstrating true chivalry, Eric sheltered Wendy with his coat from the cab to the front door.

"Thanks, Sir Walter Raleigh," she said as they took refuge under her uncle's porch. "But I'm not some exotic plant that can't stand a little rain."

He laughed. "Hardly. I'd say you're more like a desert cactus—prickly, but what's beneath the surface is worth getting skewered for."

"You pack a prickle or two yourself, Sir Walter." She couldn't help responding to his backhanded compliment with a smile. She rang the doorbell.

Uncle Mark opened it so quickly, Wendy suspected he must have been on the lookout for them. He ushered them in. "Well, for goodness' sake, honey, you didn't have to ring. It's ghastly outside." He helped Wendy out of her coat, shook it out, and then hung it up.

Before Wendy could introduce him to Eric, Aunt Lily bustled out from the kitchen, wiping her hands on the apron around her waist. Her plump face was dotted with flour, and a stray lock of her gray hair had escaped from her topknot. The heavenly aroma of apples and cinnamon wafting toward them made Wendy feel like she had come home.

"You two must be starving," Lily said. "Oh, Mark, you haven't met Eric Tremaine, have you? This is Wendy's friend from the States. Have you two eaten?" she asked.

Eric laughed. "We had lunch, Lily, but I'm sure I could handle some of your great cooking. Pleased to meet you, Mark," he added, shaking Mark's outstretched hand.

"We don't expect a meal," Wendy assured her. "In fact, Eric probably has to get over to the hospital. Right, Eric?"

"Nonsense, children," Aunt Lily protested. "I made lots of supper, hoping you would get home in time. And here you are." She hurried back to the kitchen. Wendy followed.

In the kitchen, Lily turned to her niece. "It's just so wonderful to have you turn up like this, so unexpectedly." She pulled Wendy into a swift hug.

"I've missed you and Uncle Mark." The words seemed to set off another teary session for both of them. Then Wendy added, "I was sad when Mother told me we wouldn't be coming to see you anymore."

Tears glistened in Lily's eyes. "I thought that's how it was. And what could a ten-year-old child do about that? Well, now that you've found your way to us, I hope we'll see a lot more of you, dear." Lily turned back to the stove and started dishing out plates of food. "By the way, how is your mother? Is she happy now?"

Wendy filled the kettle and set it on the stove to boil, surprised not so much by the question, but by the genuine interest she heard in her aunt's voice. "Mother moved to Alberta last year, about the time I went to work in Shadow Ridge. She has a sister and a couple of nephews there. As to her being happy, I have to be honest, Aunt Lily. I've never thought of my mother as happy. I guess her happiness ended after she lost her husband." Wendy had no desire to hurt her aunt's feelings. Naturally, Lily loved her brother and took his side, but actions always had consequences. Loving someone didn't change that.

Lily handed Wendy two food-laden plates. "Set these at the table, dear. And you can tell the men to sit down, if you would." Wendy took the plates into the dining room. When she returned, her aunt said, "Your father never wanted to leave you, dear. I want you to know that." Lily filled two more plates for her niece.

As she placed them on the table, something struck a memory chord. Her aunt had prepared all her favorite comfort foods: roast beef and mashed potatoes and gravy, with steamed baby carrots. Glancing up, she caught her aunt watching her as if waiting. "My 'favorite-est' meal in the whole world, Aunt Lily. You remembered." And they both laughed and hugged and cried some more.

Mark and Eric's appearance interrupted the nostalgic moment. Wendy and Lily broke apart, and Lily immediately took charge. "Sit anywhere you want," she told Eric, who sat opposite Mark.

"Are you girls enjoying your crying spree?" Mark asked, winking broadly at Eric. "Don't worry, son. For some reason, women cry a lot when they get together. One of those mysteries from time immemorial."

Lily shushed him, and Wendy sat down, still lost in thought. Imagine her aunt remembering her favorite dishes after all these years. *What a shame I never contacted them before this,* she thought. Eric was right about one thing: she was a grown-up now and no longer under her mother's jurisdiction.

Mark entered into a lively discussion with Eric about horses. The two men kept the conversation entertaining and light, exactly what Wendy needed. When the dinner plates were empty, she and Lily cleared the table. Lily sent her guests to the living room while she "tidied up." Minutes later she brought in a tray with mugs of coffee and a heaping plate of brownies.

To make room for the tray her aunt had brought in, Wendy picked up a photo album on the coffee table. As she flipped idly through it, one photo caught her eye. Quickly she skimmed through the pages, recognizing her mother in several.

"We were just looking at your baby pictures this evening, dear," her uncle said. He sounded almost apologetic and glanced at Lily.

"I've never seen these photos," she whispered. "We all looked so happy." Grief welled up within her for all she had lost, all that might have been. If only.

"Steven, your father, took most of them," Lily said quietly. "The ones with your father were taken during our visits with all of you. You were such a sweet child. After your parents divorced, your father spent many hours poring over these pictures."

Wendy studied them for several minutes without speaking. Conversation buzzed around her as Lily offered coffee and brownies to the men. Finally Wendy spoke. "We were a family. Why couldn't he stay?" She threw the question out as if challenging the universe to explain how this terrible event could have happened.

"I would say your father gave it his best shot," her aunt ventured hesitantly.

"You're blaming Mother?" Wendy rushed to her mother's defense. Who else could, here among her father's family? Lily looked shaken.

"There are two sides to every story," Mark said calmly.

"I guess I'm a black-and-white kind of person," Wendy said coolly.

"We spent quite a bit of time with your family when you were too young to remember, dear. We thought your mother was, well, a very insecure person. If your father came home late, even a few minutes, she thought he was seeing another woman."

"And it turned out he was," Wendy said decisively. "And it broke her heart."

The look on Mark's face registered pity, and for some reason that made Wendy angry.

Lily said quietly but with confidence, "No, Wendy, Steven never cheated on your mother. Ever. Believing something is true doesn't make it so. But Deborah's constant suspicion and distrust of him broke your father's heart."

"I guess it's just your word against Mother's." Wendy couldn't believe she was having this conversation. At this moment she devoutly wished she had never called Aunt Lily.

"And for years you've seen things only from your mother's perspective," her aunt pointed out to her as gently as possible.

"Of course I have. My father was nowhere in sight. He never spoke to me after he walked out that door." Wendy's chest tightened. "He never even wrote to me. He promised he would. But he didn't." Her last words were barely audible. "I hate him."

Silence followed that. No one seemed able to move.

Finally Eric said, "You wouldn't care so much if you did, Wendy." She glared at him but knew he was right. She had a secret reason for hanging on to her father's photograph, even after her mother had burned all the others. Wendy had hoped against hope . . . but her father had never contacted her. It hurt so much, she felt as if she was going to burst.

"I'll be right back, Wendy. Don't move," Lily said, and she went upstairs.

Mark cleared away the remaining brownies and cold coffee while his wife was gone. By the time he rejoined Eric and Wendy, Lily was entering the room. She went directly to Wendy and dropped a small bundle into her lap and then sat down close to her niece.

"I can finally give these to you, dear child. They belong to you. Your father wrote them to you after he left."

Wendy stared at the thick stack of letters, bound with a beautiful, wide red ribbon. She reached out to touch it but drew her hand back. "Why do you have them?"

"Your mother returned them to us, unopened," Aunt Lily explained. "She intercepted all Steven's attempts to contact you. Did you know that he called you on the phone almost every day for months after he left?"

Wendy shook her head, numb.

"He was never allowed to talk to you. Deborah always told him that you didn't want anything to do with him."

Wendy stared openmouthed at her aunt with a look of utter disbelief.

Lily nodded vigorously. "It's true, Wendy. You're old enough to hear the truth, even if it hurts." Lily's expression was filled with compassion. "When Steven eventually moved to Kitimat, he gave these letters to me for safekeeping. He wanted you to have them someday. I think he always hoped that you would want him back one day."

"Want *him* back? I thought he didn't want *me*." Tears filled her eyes. "Mother was protecting me from him . . . I thought he was the one . . . How can I be sure who's telling the truth?"

Lily put her arm around Wendy's shoulders and pointed to the letters. "Maybe you'll find the answer in his letters to you, my dear. I prayed that I'd be able to give them to you. They're yours. You have heard your mother's voice all these years. Now listen to your father's."

Wendy nodded, unconsciously hugging the letters to her heart.

Eric stood up. "It's getting late," he said. "I'd better get back to the hospital."

His move seemed to mobilize everyone at once, except Wendy. Mark immediately offered to drive Eric to the hospital and went to get his wallet and car keys. Lily picked up the remaining coffee mugs and took them out to the kitchen.

Alone with Wendy, Eric went to her and knelt beside her chair. "Are you okay?"

She nodded, turning to face him. "I thought . . . I don't know what to think."

"Read the letters. Don't be afraid."

"Why would I be afraid?"

"It can be scary having to change your mind about something you thought you had all figured out," he said, and he leaned over to drop a feathery kiss on her temple. Gazing down at her with a teasing sparkle in his eyes, he murmured, "In case you're wondering, that was just a 'partner's' peck. I'll be back here at nine tomorrow morning. Our flight leaves at eleven."

"I'll be ready." She gave him a watery smile.

Wendy knew before she had finished the first letter that sleep would be out of the question that night. Her father's greeting unleashed the tears she had been holding back. She sobbed all the way through it. *My Dear Little Daydreamer,* he began. *The first thing I want to tell you is that I love you very much. Even though your mother and I have decided not to live together anymore, it doesn't mean that you and I won't see each other. . . .* The letters started on a bright note, with his hopes to get together with her often. After a time, realizing that his wife was not going to allow him access to Wendy, he became more pessimistic.

After a year, the letters became less frequent. Finally he told her that he was being transferred to a job in Kitimat. *But,* he added, *I will keep in touch with Aunt Lily. She will always know where I am and will give me news of you if she can. I'm sorry for so much, my little Wendy. I left your mother because I thought she would be happier without me. I thought I could still be a part of your life, but I was wrong.*

I hope that someday you will want to see me again. Please believe that I won't ever stop loving you. I loved your mother with all my heart, too, but she couldn't believe me. Love and trust must go hand in hand, and if you learn that, you will live a full and happy life, my daughter. Please forgive me for not being a better father.

Wendy carefully put the final letter down. Her father's words had given her a picture of him she had never seen before. Now, for the first time in her life, she was seeing her father through the eyes of an adult. The unfeeling, treacherous monster her mother had created in Wendy's mind had never existed. Steven

Hunt was nothing more than a human being, flawed like the rest of the human race.

Knowing that her mother had kept Wendy from her father's love opened another can of worms. Intimate acquaintance with her mother's pain for so many years enabled Wendy to understand why Deborah had done it. But now Wendy realized that her mother's beliefs were baseless. Her mother's problem had been her inability to trust her husband's love. Her father had been unable to cope with his wife's relentless suspicions and accusations. Wendy had heard them all her life. How much had her resulting mind-set hurt her own relationships, even with Richard?

Something else occurred to her in those early-morning hours.

As efficient, capable, and responsible as she had become in her profession, where her parents' divorce was concerned, she was still a child. She blamed herself. Now, because of the letters, she understood that her parents' problems had nothing to do with her. They had simply had "irreconcilable differences." In this day and age, it happened all the time.

Most important, she now knew that her father had not merely forgotten her. He had loved her, wanted to be in her life, wanted to see her again. The words she had longed to hear for years were in those letters, filling the hole in her heart. The healing could begin. As slivers of daylight stole silently into the room, Wendy slept.

Chapter Eleven

Wendy studied her reflection carefully the next morning. The damage from several hours of crying on top of less than two hours of sleep would take a week at a spa to repair. But the puffy eyes and blotchy cheeks still told little of the inward upheaval she had experienced last night. She sighed. Makeup could conceal only so much.

Aunt Lily greeted her with her usual warmth and hovered like a mother hen. The huge breakfast she had prepared made yesterday's seem like bread and water. Wendy's stomach balked at the eggs, bacon, and pancakes her aunt set in front of her. It was a wonder Uncle Mark wasn't the size of an elephant if he ate this way every morning.

As if he had read her mind, Mark winked at her and said, "Your Aunt Lily doesn't cook like this when we're alone." Had he said it to let Wendy know that her aunt was trying to show her affection? Wendy's already swollen eyes stung with unshed tears. How could there be any left after last night's deluge?

She hated to disappoint her aunt, who stood waiting to fill her plate. "I'm afraid my appetite won't do justice to your wonderful cooking, Aunt Lily," she began. But when she saw the disappointment in her aunt's eyes, she hastened to add, "Could I start with scrambled eggs and one pancake—a small one?" Beaming, Lily dished out a generous helping of eggs and a stack of three pancakes. She looked so pleased, Wendy didn't have the heart to say anything more.

The doorbell rang. "That must be Eric," Lily said. As Mark went to let him in, she added, "We'll be taking you two to the airport to see you off. Eric and Mark arranged it last night. Among other things," she added mysteriously, but she did not go into specifics. Lily heaped an astonishing amount of food onto another plate and put it beside Wendy's.

"Here we are," said Mark, returning to the kitchen with Eric behind him. As Wendy contemplated how she was going to make her pancakes disappear without eating them, Eric greeted her aunt with a peck on the cheek.

Blushing, she said, "You delightful man. Now sit down and eat up. Your plate is on the table." She wiped her hands on her apron and began to put together another batch of pancake batter.

Aunt Lily has officially joined the ranks of the Eric Tremaine fan club, Wendy decided.

While Mark and Lily carried on a lively discussion about pancake flipping and how well the eggs should be cooked, Eric sat down in front of the plate Lily had given him. Aware of his intense gaze perusing her shipwrecked face, Wendy looked away. Thankfully, he said nothing except, "Good morning, Wendy," before digging into his food. It astonished her that he could put away so much and still have a body like—she stopped her thoughts right there and stared down at the plate in front of her.

He glanced over at her untouched pancakes several times before finally asking, "Do you mind?" She shook her head. He lifted them as one onto his own plate. "I didn't think so." After adding more syrup, he said in a low voice for her ears alone, "You look terrible."

She felt terrible.

* * *

Their departure at the airport proved to be an emotional round of good-byes, and it was all Wendy could do to keep her tears at bay. She was afraid if she let them go, she'd never be able to rein them in again, so she tried to detach herself from what was happening around her. She hugged Aunt Lily, promising to come again. Uncle Mark embraced her warmly and whispered, "Call us anytime, dear. You're family, don't forget."

By the time she and Eric had passed through security and found their gate, her head felt like it was about to explode. At that moment, she would have sold her soul for two aspirin.

"What are you looking for?" Eric asked while watching her rummage through her handbag.

"Aspirin," she said. "You wouldn't happen to have one in your back pocket, would you? I have a splitting headache."

"Sorry," he said.

She found his apologetic manner endearing, but an aspirin would have won him a lot more points.

"Here's a gift shop," he added, leading her in. "I see a few over-the-counter drugs in the back." Wendy found a tiny aspirin bottle holding eight tablets for $3.50—highway robbery. Nevertheless, she made the purchase and he bought her a bottle of apple juice to wash down the pills.

Eric led her back to a seat in the waiting area. She sat down and said, "So, how's Horace doing? Did he get discharged okay? How about transport home?"

"He's doing great. He's already back home, safe and sound—no thanks to me." He shook his head. "I never should have brought him to Shadow Ridge." Then he turned to watch Wendy for a few moments. "For that matter, I never should have talked to you in the hospital. Now you're involved in this mess too."

"Ouch. Please. My head already feels like it's under the weight of the world. I can't handle your regrets too."

"Sorry. Forgive my overdeveloped sense of responsibility. Why don't you take a couple of those pills and sleep it off? You obviously didn't get much rest last night."

"No, I didn't. And yes, I will, thank you, although I don't expect to get much sleep on that puddle jumper we're flying in. The propeller engine is so loud, you can't hear anything else. Plus it makes the plane vibrate."

"I see what you mean about not being able to handle more pain. You have enough already."

"Getting back to your overdeveloped sense of responsibility, I just want to say that too many men don't have one, but too much of a good thing is . . . I mean, you aren't responsible for everything and everyone, that's all," she told him. Then she tossed back two aspirin with a gulp of juice and closed her eyes. After a minute or two, her head drooped against his shoulder. Eric rested his head against hers.

"Tell me about your family," she said after a long silence.

"I thought you were asleep. How's your headache?"

"Still there but better." She sat up straight and opened her eyes. "Thanks for your shoulder. So, tell me about your family," she repeated. "Your mother and father and Scott."

He stretched out his legs and readjusted his position in the chair. "My—our—mother is still alive. My father died when I was six. I really don't remember him."

"I'm sorry," Wendy said softly, thinking of her own father. "Other brothers or sisters?"

"I was their only child," he answered. "But my mother married Allen Ellerslie when I was seven. Scott came along a year later. Unfortunately, I never got along with my stepfather."

"Why not?"

"Are you sure you want to delve into this right now? Your head, remember?"

"Your family lore might distract me from my pain. Please go on. Why couldn't you get along with your stepfather? Was he abusive? Too strict? Mean?"

"None of the above. He was a good man, actually. After a while he basically ignored me. I wanted a father, but he just wanted a wife. My mother doted on him. He was her world. When he died nine years later, Scott filled the void for her."

"So you more or less lost your mother's attention twice—first to your stepfather and then to Scott?"

"I'm making it sound like I was neglected. It was partly my own fault. After my father died, I didn't understand my mother's loneliness. A child can't replace a spouse. But when she remarried, I guess in my childish mind I decided she was choosing Allen over me. I was horrible. I rebelled, misbehaved, and did everything I could to sabotage them." He paused.

"Go on," Wendy said. She could see that Eric was remembering with regret. She wished she could take away the sadness in his eyes.

"You can imagine that Allen and I didn't have the best father-son relationship. It's a shame, too, because I know now that he was a good man. In the beginning he tried to be my friend, but I kept him at a surly distance. I feel bad that I never got a chance to tell him all that before he died. I more or less shot myself in the foot as far as family relationships went."

A few passengers had drifted into the waiting area. Wendy kept her eye on the flight agent at the desk, who appeared to be waiting for a signal to begin boarding passengers. Their plane was sitting on the tarmac, dwarfed by the big jets. "I think we're going to be going soon," she said. "Talk now because we won't be able to once we're in the air. I want to hear more." She smiled. "And my headache's pretty much gone now."

"I'm glad." He said it with a tenderness that touched her. "Where was I?"

"You were a boy of seven, jealous of the man who came between you and your mother," she said. "You didn't understand all that then. It must have been very lonely for you."

He raised his eyebrows and said, "So you not only listen, you give a free analysis?"

She grinned. "Just part of the friendly Canadian way. Go on."

"It was lonely for a few years," he admitted. "Then, when I was a teenager, Horace arrived. He happened onto the ranch one day, looking for work. He was down on his luck and looked like the worst kind of bum, but Allen saw beyond all that and decided to hire him. Horace proved to be an invaluable foreman, and the timing was providential—within a year, Allen was dead. Horace had to teach me how to run the ranch after that. I was barely sixteen. Horace patiently guided me through the ins and outs of ranching, hiring and firing, and doing the books. For a long time, even though I was ostensibly the man giving the orders, I was standing on his shoulders."

"That explains your closeness with Horace," Wendy said, thinking about the loss of a father she and Eric had in common. "So you became the head of the household at the tender age of sixteen, when most boys are out having fun, while your mom raised young Scott. I bet he looked up to you—a lot," she mused aloud.

"Yeah, I guess he did. Only I became—"

"His tyrannical big brother?"

He nodded. "Scott's favorite nickname for me, apparently."

Wendy smiled knowingly—but sympathetically this time. She saw that it was nearly time to board their plane and decided to use the restroom one more time. She hurried to the nearest one.

As soon as she returned, they walked out to a small red and white plane. Their bags were loaded underneath, and they had to stoop to climb in. Wendy checked the tickets and slid into her seat, feeling pushed up against the window. They were two rows behind the cockpit, which was separated from the passengers by a simple curtain.

The plane seated about twenty, and three more passengers embarked after them. After they had buckled their seat belts, Wendy said, "Scott adored you, you know."

Eric gave her a sharp look. "I beg your pardon?"

"When he was a boy, you were his hero, his idol. All he ever wanted was to grow up to be just like you." Eric looked skeptical. "But he told me that after his father died, you began to change. That you got tougher on him than he expected his big brother to be."

"I knew firsthand that, without a dad, he needed firm guidance."

"He felt he could never measure up to your standards."

"Is that what he told you?"

"He also told me that you were so good at everything, you didn't need anyone, including him."

The words dangled in the air. Wendy took a breath. There was something else Eric needed to hear. "Scott felt that, with you at the helm, neither the ranch nor your mother really needed a screw-up like him in Rosewood, so he left. The ironic thing is that the whole time I knew him in Shadow Ridge, he kept telling me about how proud you'd be when he became a success on his own. All he wanted was your approval."

Eric gave her a withering glance. "Really," he said sarcastically. "You seem to have Scott and me all figured out."

"Thank you," she said, refusing to take the bait. "I know whereof I speak, Mr. Tremaine. All my life I've wanted to hear my father tell me he loved me and was proud of me, but I acted like I hated him." She sniffed. "I finally got my wish at Aunt Lily's." She had to stop, or she'd start bawling again.

Eric put an arm around her shoulders and drew her close. "Oh, Wendy."

She rested her head against him, just for a moment. "Love makes fools of us all," she murmured.

"Ain't that the truth?" Eric agreed.

Wendy felt so comfortable, she decided it couldn't hurt to stay where she was. And, despite the plane's noise and vibration, she was already drifting into an exhausted slumber.

Chapter Twelve

Joe Chandler was pacing at the gate when the plane landed.

"I see your protector is awaiting your safe arrival," Eric commented to Wendy, watching the doctor from the window of the plane as it taxied to a halt.

"Hmm. To tell the truth, I'm a little afraid of him. I think he's jealous of you."

"That's perfect. It makes my job easier."

"Your job?"

He grinned engagingly. "Yes, my self-appointed task of keeping you out of harm's way until Scott's found. Oops. Did I just see your hackles rise?"

She couldn't help laughing, and she was still smiling when they exited the plane. Joe's scowl greeted her when they picked up their bags.

"How nice of you to meet us," Eric said to him, taking Wendy's arm in his. They walked into the airport, a small enterprise with only one ticket counter.

Joe ignored Eric. "Are you okay, Wendy?"

"Of course I am, Joe. And Horace is doing well, too, by the way."

"Good. Dr. Thomas asked me to pick you up." Joe looked pointedly at Eric, who merely tightened his grip on Wendy's arm and pulled her closer to his side.

"Thanks, Dr. Chandler," Eric said easily. "That's very kind of both of you."

From the scowl on Joe's face, Wendy could tell he was annoyed; he had not anticipated picking up Eric. To avoid escalating the tension between the two men, Wendy extricated herself from Eric's protective arm and moved ahead of him.

Joe fell into step beside Wendy, leaving Eric a pace or two behind.

"I think I'll pop in at the hospital before I go home," Wendy said, and she turned around to address Eric. "Call me later when you get settled, okay . . . partner?"

"I will," he said. "Could you slow down, you two? Chandler, I need to ask you about something."

Joe waited for Eric to catch up. "What is it, Tremaine?"

"I understand you were the one who told Wendy that Scott Ellerslie had left Shadow Ridge. Is that correct?" Clearly surprised at the question, Joe glanced warily around the empty terminal. Was he looking to see if anyone was listening?

Joe exhaled loudly. "So?"

Eric made no attempt to hide his impatience. "Did you actually know that Scott left town, or did someone else tell you he had gone?"

Joe was clearly flustered, although why the simple question should be so troublesome puzzled Wendy. He acted as if he was hiding something, and that bothered her.

"Joe, you told me he left. Who told *you*?" Wendy pressed.

"What does it matter, Wendy? Your precious boyfriend up and left you." He glared at Eric. "Constable Ganzer told me," he growled. "He told me the day after Whitefoot called me down to a godforsaken beach at the foot of a cliff with some crazy story about Ellerslie's being hurt. There was nothing there. Whitefoot was probably drunk."

Wendy's eyes narrowed at the ugly remark. Joe glanced from one to the other, his face red. "Are you coming or not?" he asked.

She had no other way home, so she nodded. Joe went ahead to a pickup.

"That was a rather revealing conversation, wouldn't you say?" Eric asked her, as the two of them followed Joe.

She nodded. "Who'd have thought . . . ?" They had reached the vehicle, and Eric deliberately climbed in first, beside Joe. He then patted the seat next to him and grinned at Wendy. She got in and shut the door.

Tense silence filled the truck until Joe stopped in front of the hospital. "I assume you can both make it from here," he said, clearly angry.

Wendy left the vehicle, and Eric followed her. When Joe drove off, Eric said, "I'll shower and change at the motel. Then I'm going to see Quentin. We—as in he and I, not you and I—may investigate the sawmill. Don't worry—I'll keep you informed." His face grew serious. "I want to state this for the record, whether it's being 'tyrannical' or not. Wendy, I don't want you at that sawmill again." She opened her mouth in protest, but he held up a hand to stop her. "Remember what happened to you last time?"

She closed her mouth. "Good point," she said.

"That's better. Now, are you working tomorrow?"

"I start graveyard shift tonight."

"Then you get some sleep," he said. "I hope you'll give your notice soon, so you can get out of here."

"More and more I see what Scott meant about your taking over," Wendy muttered, but she was too tired to argue. "Never mind, I agree," she said. She laughed at his surprised expression. "About the nap, anyway." She took her bag from him and left him to find his own way to the motel. After some sleep and a few more aspirin to kill the pain in her head, she would be able to put up a better fight. Unfortunately, she was becoming quite reluctant to fight Eric. It was nice having someone worry and fuss over her, to feel that her welfare was the most important thing on his mind.

Connie met Wendy walking into the residence. "Well, I see you still have to have all the men," she said sarcastically. "Isn't one enough for you?"

"What are you talking about, Connie?" Wendy asked, weary of Connie's jealousy. Was this how her mother had been with her father?

"I saw that Joe went to the trouble of picking you up at the airport, but you brought Eric *back* with you." *That picture window upstairs overlooking the whole town didn't miss much,* Wendy thought.

"For the last time, Connie, I don't have any feelings for Joe Chandler. If he doesn't like you, it's not my fault."

"Whatever. How can I compete with you? You're so chirpy, and cute, and . . . and—" Connie burst into tears. "I'll never get anyone to love me."

Not if you're so prickly all the time. Then Wendy remembered that Eric had compared *her* to a desert cactus. Reaching out in compassion to a fellow thorny person, she said, "Connie, you underrate yourself." Wendy patted her awkwardly. "And you definitely *over*rate me," she added dryly.

Connie sniffed loudly. Once again, her mood changed like lightning. "You're always right, aren't you, Wendy?" she said in a cold, hard voice. "Maybe I'll go after Eric and see how *you* like it." Abruptly, she brushed past Wendy and left her standing alone in the foyer, feeling like a fool.

Wendy's exhaustion caught up with her, and she slept until 9:30. She had no time to do anything more than get ready for work. She did spare a few thoughts for Eric. What had he done all day? Was anything up? She tried calling the motel, but he wasn't in. *No news was good news,* she told herself. She had no choice but to report for work, even if, at this point, she hated being left out of the loop.

Eric and his doings took a backseat to her duties that night. With three deliveries, one bar brawl, and a cardiac arrest, she and Helen were kept so busy, it was morning before she realized it. Connie and Janet came on to relieve them.

Back at the residence, almost as soon as she pulled the covers up over her head to shut out the light, sleep claimed her again. When she finally surfaced, it was 2:00 in the afternoon.

She awoke to the sound of a telephone ringing. Disoriented at first, it took her a minute to remember she was back in her own room at Shadow Ridge and not in Aunt Lily's frilly white guestroom in Vancouver. She trudged down the hall to answer the phone.

Eric was on the other end. "What took you so long? Are you going to sleep your life away?" He sounded annoyingly cheerful.

"Well, a few hours of it, I thought. What have you been up to? I called the motel last night, but you weren't there."

"Do I detect a note of suspicion, perhaps a hint of jealousy?"

"Absolutely not. Neither. I'm just not a morning person, Eric. This is morning to me."

"'Nuff said. Are you dressed? I mean that in the nicest, most innocent way."

"No . . . that is, not in street clothes. I'm still in my pajamas— I mean, nightie—" She broke off, as embarrassed as if she were completely exposed to his view. She even tried to fix her hair a little and pulled her robe tighter before she rolled her eyes in disgust at her idiocy.

"You probably look beautiful, Wendy, but you'd better get dressed so I can concentrate on our project. Meet me at Meg's Café in half an hour?"

Despite her desire to resist his ridiculous flattery, Wendy couldn't stop the smile from spreading across her face. "I'll meet you there in forty-five minutes," she said, just to exert her own will.

"That's fine," he said, taking the wind out of her sails.

"Men!" she muttered as she hung up. "I suppose he thinks my heart was racing and my palms were sweaty just talking to him on the phone." She rubbed her damp palms together and waited several seconds for her pulse to settle down. As she walked back to her room, a soft smile stole across her face.

She pulled on a pink sweater that perfectly complemented her heather gray slacks and automatically applied lip gloss.

At 2:45 on a Monday afternoon, Meg's Café was practically deserted, but Wendy slipped in unnoticed just as someone else was leaving. Glancing around, she saw Eric engaged in what looked like a very serious conversation with John Ganzer. About to make herself known, she stopped cold at Eric's angry voice.

"She doesn't know. It's safer that way."

The constable laughed—a harsh, mocking laugh. "I doubt that. Women find these things out. Just keep her out of my way, Tremaine. I've worked too hard and too long on this to let some woman ruin it, even if she is your girlfriend."

Eric reached over and grabbed Ganzer's collar, pulling him half out of his seat and facing him nose to nose. "If you touch a hair on her head, you will answer to me," he growled. "I don't care if you're the law or even the king of Canada." Eric let him go as if he couldn't stand touching him.

John Ganzer shoved his chair back nonchalantly and stood up. "If you don't want to see someone you care about get hurt, keep out of my way." He stopped. "And just for future reference, Tremaine, you should know that Canada has a prime minister, not a king."

When he spotted Wendy approaching, Ganzer said, "A word to the wise, which I hope you are, Miss Hunt." He looked at her coldly. "Stop playing constable, and keep your day job." He turned to leave.

As the door shut behind him, Wendy stared at his retreating figure through the window, watching silently until he disappeared from view. She then turned to Eric. His face was inscrutable.

"What was that all about, Eric? It sounded as if he was threatening you. And me too."

Eric didn't invite her to sit down. He pushed the table away, stood up, and threw down a bill. "The man watches too many cop shows. He's being overly dramatic for effect."

"Well, it's working. I'm affected. But I want to know what I'm not supposed to know."

To her relief, that elicited a grin, not a frown, from him. "Of course you want to know. You're a woman." As he said it, his smile faded, and desire leaped into his eyes. But as quickly as she saw it flame, it was gone, replaced with a bleak coldness. "The fact is—and I agree with Ganzer about this—there is something going on here in Shadow Ridge, and I want you safely out of it."

"What did he tell you?"

"He told me he's a special agent assigned by the RCMP to investigate this local detachment for corruption and possible criminal activity, and he wants us out of the way," Eric said.

Wendy's eyes widened in surprise.

Eric nodded. "I know. It's almost the same thing LeBoeuf told us."

"Then who's lying?"

"Is anyone around here telling the truth?" He stared out the window as if looking for an answer. Something in his manner bothered her. It was as if he had withdrawn from her. "What are your plans?" he asked politely, his expression blank.

"*My* plans?" she echoed stupidly. She stared at him, trying to find something in his face that looked familiar. He had suddenly become a stranger she might have just met. What had happened to *their* plans?

The silence lengthened. She waited. When she had his attention again, she said, "*My* plan at this moment is to visit Opal and Quentin. Would you care to share yours with me?"

He opened his mouth as if rising to the bait, but after a moment of hesitation, he checked his watch and shrugged. "We should go now, before it looks like we're angling for more of Opal's home cooking."

"*We?* Are you sure? I wouldn't want to keep you from more important business." She turned around to march out of the café before he could see the hurt in her face.

He followed her out. Without a word he escorted her to his truck, opened the passenger door, and slammed it shut behind her. "Don't be silly," he told her as if she had blown their exchange out of all proportion.

She hoped that was the case, but as she studied his granite profile, she could swear she was not overreacting. She was confused. Something had happened in the time between his phone call to her at the residence and her arrival at the café. John Ganzer had happened. Whatever he had told Eric had caused him to withdraw from her as completely as the ocean from the shore at low tide.

She had seen the spark of desire in Eric's eyes. She hadn't imagined it, surely. Nevertheless, she knew he was hiding something. Eric's look reminded her of Richard, when she had caught him with Cindy. Her heart was heavy on the short drive to the Whitefoots'. In fact, neither of them spoke.

The cabin looked deserted when Eric pulled up in front. No smoke curled from the chimney. No vehicle was in sight.

"It's a little cool for no fire," commented Wendy. She knocked loudly on the front door. "Quentin must be out, and maybe Opal's napping."

After several moments with no response, Wendy was about to suggest they come back another time. She turned to Eric but stopped abruptly.

"What is it?" he asked quickly. "Did you hear something?"

"I did." She opened the door and called in. "Hello? Quentin? Opal?" She walked in, Eric close on her heels. They both stopped to listen.

"It's coming from the bedroom. I think it's Opal," Wendy said, and she hurried through the door. Opal was lying on the bed, writhing and panting in obvious distress. "Opal! What's wrong? It's the baby, isn't it? It's coming!" Wendy was at her side in seconds, feeling her abdomen while Opal groaned.

Eric watched the two women with a question in his eyes. Wendy nodded. "She's in labor. She needs to get to the hospital. Can you carry her to the truck?"

Eric came closer, but Opal put up a hand. "No!" she gasped. "The baby's coming now. Wendy, help me!"

Eric stopped midstep and looked at Wendy. "Is there time?"

"I'm not sure. Phone the clinic. Ask whoever's on to bring the ambulance and the emergency-delivery pack. Then bring me as many towels as you can find and put some water on the stove to boil," Wendy told him. She quickly went to scrub her hands thoroughly and then returned to Opal. "I'm going to examine you, Opal, to see how close you are to delivery, okay?"

Opal nodded and relaxed a bit. The contraction was over, and Wendy did the examination. The delivery was imminent. Too late to go to the hospital. She propped Opal up on several pillows and positioned her legs better. Opal was still in her nightclothes, which meant she had probably been in labor all day. Where was Quentin?

Eric came back into the room with a handful of towels. "The ambulance is on its way. Where do you want these?" His calm manner was comforting to both women.

Wendy took a deep breath. "Put them there," she said, indicating a spot on the bed. Wendy placed the biggest towel under Opal. "Her water broke," she explained to Eric, assuming he would know what she was talking about.

"I see," he said, sounding like a doctor. "What should I do with the boiling water?"

"Oh, I don't know. Make some tea. You always boil water when a baby is coming," she snapped.

He laughed, and for a moment Wendy glimpsed the old Eric. Hope surged in her heart, but she had no time to think about Eric, because another contraction tore into Opal.

"Opal, just breathe, like this," Wendy instructed, panting until she felt almost light-headed. Between pushing and panting,

Opal got through the contraction. Wendy prayed that the ambulance would be there soon.

Opal sank back into the pillows when the contraction ended and lay as still as death, her eyes closed. Wendy quickly took a small towel, moistened it, and gently wiped Opal's face, neck, and arms. She looked so young, so vulnerable, lying there, exhausted from her labor.

"Where is Quentin?" Eric asked, startling Wendy. He had been watching for the ambulance. She shrugged.

"He went to Skidigate today to pick up some slate," breathed Opal. "He should have been back by now."

"Were you in labor when he left, Opal?" Wendy asked.

Opal shook her head. "I wasn't supposed to have this baby for another three weeks."

"Babies come when they're ready, Opal. This little one's in a big hurry. Don't worry. You're doing fine."

Wendy knew she sounded calmer than she felt. At that moment, Eric caught her eye. As if he knew what was really going on inside her, he half smiled and nodded reassuringly. Her heart swelled with encouragement, as well as hope—hope that the Eric she had come to know and love was still there. She made a mental note to grab him after this was over and not let him go until they had talked this through. That intimate image sent waves of delicious anticipation coursing through her, but Opal's next contraction completely pushed those feelings aside.

Just as it subsided, they heard the ambulance arrive. Eric dashed to fling open the door, and Wendy leaned down to Opal. "It's the doctor, Opal. Everything will be just fine now."

Eric returned, followed by Joe Chandler, who was carrying a black bag in one hand and a wrapped bundle in the other. Wendy stepped back to give him room. "Joe, am I glad to see you! Opal's fully dilated, and she's pushing. You can scrub up in there," she told him, pointing to the bathroom. "Hurry."

Joe nodded, quickly shed his coat, scrubbed his hands, and opened the emergency-delivery kit. He flung two sterile drapes over Opal's legs and one across her belly. Another he put under her bottom. Wendy cleared a sizable space on the bureau beside him and spread the rest of the kit out on it. Joe put on gloves, and Wendy slipped a sterile gown over his clothes. She automatically reached around his waist to grab the tie to close the back of the gown. Their eyes met. Wendy instinctively shrank back from the intensity of desire she saw there.

By the time Opal's next contraction came, the tiny bedroom was transformed into a remarkable facsimile of a hospital delivery room.

"Okay, Opal, let's see you push with your next contraction," Joe instructed. "We need to get this baby down a bit lower."

Following Wendy's earlier instructions, Opal pushed and panted valiantly. Together, the three worked through two more contractions before Joe finally, triumphantly shouted, "Stop pushing, now—here it comes!"

With a gush of fluid, the baby emerged, its head covered in a mat of jet black hair. Wrinkled and wet, the infant gave its first cry, loud, piercing, and reassuring. Opal, so close to complete exhaustion a moment ago, sat up with an angelic smile of joy on her face and tears streaming down her cheeks.

"It's a boy!" exclaimed Joe, placing the baby on Opal's stomach. Tenderly, she touched him, making first contact with the tiny being she had waited so long to meet face-to-face.

Joe was clamping the baby's umbilical cord when Quentin barged into the bedroom. "What's going on here? Why's the ambulance—?" He stopped when he saw Opal and the baby. "Wash your hands. You can cut the cord if you want to," Joe said to Quentin.

The native looked at Wendy, who took him to the bathroom sink. "Opal's just fine, Quent. You don't have to do this if you don't want to, but some fathers find it significant."

He just nodded, washed his hands thoroughly, and dried them on the sterile towel Wendy handed him. His fierce pride barely concealed, Quentin took the scissors and cut where Joe indicated. He managed to stay on his feet and finish his task, but Wendy quickly took the scissors from him and guided him to a safe place to sit. She wrapped the baby in a soft blanket and placed him in Opal's arms. The eager mother promptly unwrapped him and counted every digit, as Quentin looked on protectively.

"Give her five units of IV Synto, Wendy," Joe ordered, to help deliver the afterbirth. She had already drawn it up and administered it immediately. "I'll check the baby, and then we'd better get them all to the hospital." Satisfied after a cursory examination of the infant, Joe handed him to Quentin with a smile. "I'll check him out more thoroughly at the hospital, but he looks fine and healthy to me."

It amazed Wendy how an experience like childbirth could bring enemies together so fast. Whatever she felt about Joe personally, she had to admit he had been nothing less than extremely efficient and competent today. She could see from Quentin's face that he, too, was struggling with his distrust of Joe, weighing it against the birth of his son.

"Thanks, Doc," Quentin said finally, and he held out his hand.

Joe shook it and smiled. "Thank Wendy. In fact, if I hadn't been here, she would have done a fine job all by herself." Before he left the room, he took his time giving Wendy another hot look that set off warning bells in her head. She averted her face and busied herself with Opal's care.

"Thanks for all your help, Wendy," Opal said in a tired voice. "I was so afraid until you came."

Eyes filling, Wendy hugged the girl. "You're very welcome. I'm just glad I didn't sleep any later than I did. Which reminds me, have you seen Eric?"

Quentin pointed to the kitchen and grinned. "I wonder why the thought of not sleeping reminds you of Eric."

Wendy blushed.

Quentin laughed. "For some strange reason, I think he's making tea. Why don't I go show him the results of not sleeping?" He winked broadly at Wendy. "I'll bring him back to you."

"Don't hurry. I want to give Opal a sponge bath and change

her clothes," she told Quentin, who nodded and left to show off his son.

Within a few minutes, Wendy had given Opal a quick bed bath and changed her nightshirt. Joe came back with the stretcher to transfer Opal. When Quentin didn't come at Joe's call, Wendy went to get him. Something made her stop outside the kitchen door.

"Are you sure it's true, Eric? You remember Scott said not to trust the cops."

"I'm not sure I believe him, Quent, but if my brother is still alive, I want to do everything I can to keep it that way."

"Does Wendy know?"

"No," was Eric's answer.

Silence followed. Wendy imagined Eric shaking his head. What didn't she know? Something everybody else did, apparently. Something Eric couldn't trust her with. Something he was determined to keep from her.

"Wendy?" Eric found her rooted to the spot just outside the kitchen, her expression grim.

"Will you or will you not tell me what John Ganzer told you?" she demanded.

Eric looked as if he had just eaten something distasteful. He seemed unable to look her in the eye, something he had never had trouble doing until now. Slowly he shook his head. "I can't, Wendy. It's for your own good. I promise—"

"Stop right there, Mr. Tremaine." Wendy held up a hand as if to ward off a blow. "Don't make any promises to me. I've had enough broken promises from men to last forever." With that, she spun around and walked stiffly away from Eric Tremaine.

Chapter Thirteen

Back in the residence at last, Wendy was surprised to discover it was barely seven o'clock. She had stayed at the Whitefoots' after everyone, including Eric, had left. She'd wanted to change Opal's bed and tidy up as best she could. Also, she had needed to be alone.

Now she felt cold to her very bones, but she knew this coldness would not be relieved with warm clothing. Why was she so easily taken in by a handsome face and charming exterior?

Not liking her thoughts and feeling some weak pangs of hunger, she rummaged through the kitchen cupboards. Eventually she found fixings for tomato soup and a peanut butter sandwich. Sitting at the kitchen table gave her a good view of the hospital's backside, the main part of town, the wharf, and the police station. Idly she gazed out the window and watched as twilight crept into the sleepy village.

A movement out of the corner of her eye caught her attention. Two people walked down the main street into her view. She recognized one of them immediately—she would recognize Eric anywhere. The other person was shorter, female. . . . *Connie!*

Eric's head was bent close to hers, as if he were hanging on every word she said.

Wendy lost sight of the couple, and she wasn't sure if they were coming to the residence or had some other destination in mind. *Eric and Connie?* Wendy gasped at the pain it caused her to think of Eric with someone else. She felt a primitive urge to scratch Connie's eyes out. *No man is worth this pain,* her mother's voice counseled her. *But I love him,* her heart answered, drowning out all the wisdom her mind tried to offer. *How can you love a man you can't trust?* her mother would have demanded heatedly. Wendy had no answer.

When the pair did not appear at the residence, Wendy joined Janet in the living room. She and some other nurses were making decorations for the Spring Social. Up until then, Wendy had been looking forward to the festivities, especially the thought of possibly dancing with Eric if he was still in town. Despite recent hints about his untrustworthiness, she couldn't suppress the tingle of desire that tripped along her nerves as she imagined his arms around her. Tears threatened to spill out as she began stringing popcorn.

"Wendy, help me with the coffee," Janet ordered, getting up and pulling Wendy out of her chair. She had no choice but to follow Janet out to the kitchen.

"Now, what happened to you today? You look like you've lost your best friend."

Wendy hung her head.

"Did you and Eric have a fight? Is that it?" Janet persisted, undaunted by Wendy's silent shaking of her head.

In the face of Janet's unflinching gaze, Wendy nodded, unable to keep her tears in check. They rolled silently down her cheeks. "Sort of. We were supposed to be partners. He knows something important but won't tell me."

Janet's laughter sobered Wendy. "Would you please listen to yourself?" she said, shaking her head.

"What's wrong with me, Janet? I have been crying more this past week than I have in years. I'm upset because my father wrote me letters I never got, I want to scratch Connie's eyes out, and Eric is keeping a secret from me."

"Your father wrote you letters?"

Wendy nodded. "I stayed with my Aunt Lily when I was in Vancouver, and she gave me a stack of letters my father had written to me that my mother had sent back unopened. I never knew he still cared about me."

Janet whistled softly. "Well, that alone is enough for a crying jag. But scratching Connie's eyes out? Something tells me that has to do with Eric. Am I right?"

Again the nod. "I have delivered babies, run IV drips, made life-and-death judgments, but I can't seem to fall in love sensibly. How do you do it?"

Janet laughed. "In the first place, I like men—I don't fall in love with them." Janet pointed at Wendy. "You, on the other hand, fall hard and deep, and you picked a bad one the last time." She paused, as if weighing her words. "I'm here to tell you, Chicken Little, that Eric Tremaine is one of the good guys."

Wendy shook her head vigorously, denying Janet's words. "I just saw him and Connie walking down Main Street, as close as . . . well, close together."

"Now I understand about the scratching part. Which leaves Eric's secret. Did he say why he wouldn't tell you?"

"He said something about it being for my own good," Wendy mumbled.

"I see. Don't you believe him?"

"What?"

"You heard me. Don't you believe that he would try to protect you? Or is he just another jerk? You have to decide."

Wendy recoiled from her friend's blunt words. "It's not that simple," she said. "When I met Eric at Meg's Café this afternoon, he was talking to John Ganzer. After that, Eric suddenly seemed to be a total stranger. When he looked at me, it was as if we were nodding acquaintances, nothing more. Then, there's Connie," she added, feeling a knot in her stomach.

Janet dismissed Connie with a snort. "Forget the other-woman angle, Wendy. Just do me one favor?"

Wendy shook her head but then nodded. "Maybe."

"Give Eric a chance to explain."

"I was afraid you were going to say something like that."

"Wendy, I know men better than you do. You've spent too many years listening to your mother tell you that all males are devils and that lying and deception is their stock-in-trade. Eric Tremaine is not that kind of man. I'd stake my reputation on it."

"Your reputation?" Wendy said with a smile. "As a man-hunter, you mean?"

"That's the one," Janet agreed cheerfully. "It's also that experience that gives me the edge over you right now, you baby." Janet hugged Wendy quickly and then turned her toward the phone. "Now, call him. If he's worth tears, he's worth talking to. He's the only one who can answer your doubts. Trust me." Janet pushed Wendy in the direction of the phone at the end of the corridor, waiting till she saw Wendy pick up the receiver. She gave her a thumbs-up signal and returned to the others in the living room.

Wendy almost hung up while she was waiting to be put through to Eric. Her heart was already pounding in anticipation, when a voice on the other end told her there was no answer in Eric's room. Disappointed and relieved at the same time, she had no courage left to leave a message.

As soon as she walked into the living room, Janet looked up expectantly. Wendy shook her head and casually took up her popcorn string. She hoped no one noticed her trembling fingers. "Anyone know where Connie is tonight?" she asked as nonchalantly as she could manage.

Shirley spoke up. "She said something about a big date to-night. I'm so glad for her. She's been so lonely here," she added, completely unaware of the pain shooting through Wendy's heart.

* * *

By Thursday morning, Wendy had nearly lost track of what day it was. She even wondered if Eric had left Shadow Ridge while she was sleeping. But Janet informed her he was still around. Wendy went to bed and then went to work her next-to-last graveyard shift.

The following morning, Connie arrived for her shift with a gleam in her eye. Wendy was exhausted, having slept poorly over the last few days. She made the mistake of asking Connie how she was.

"Just great, Wendy. Oh, by the way, I'm meeting Eric this afternoon. We've been spending a lot of time together lately."

Wendy steeled her emotions. She didn't want to add to Connie's satisfaction. "How nice for you," she muttered, wishing to get the morning report over with and crawl under the covers of her soft, warm bed. It was just as well she hadn't reached Eric all week. Obviously, he wasn't pining away, waiting for her apology. He had probably rejoiced over shaking the Wendy Hunt albatross off his neck so easily. "What about Joe?"

"Oh, you can keep Joe. Eric is like Harrison Ford, and Joe is like . . . well, like nobody."

"Isn't Harrison Ford a little old for you?" Wendy asked caustically.

Wendy slept six hours, waking refreshed and alert, glad she had only one more night shift to work. She desperately needed to get out of the residence, walk around town, and see people. For the last six days she had felt like a creature of the darkness. Not only that, she felt as if she had missed a week of her life, a very important week. Dressing quickly, she left the residence with an almost-forgotten spring in her step. Meandering through town, she met a few people and stopped for chats along the way, feeling better by the minute.

Treating herself to supper at Meg's Café, Wendy half hoped that Eric might have a similar thought. She lingered until the café emptied, and by the time she emerged, the sun had dipped low on the horizon. Main Street rolled up at six every evening, and Wendy saw only the odd solitary person as she ambled aimlessly. After a while she realized she was close to the waterfront. She followed the sound of the waves lapping against the wharf posts right out to the end of the dock, where a warehouse stood.

Noticing several crates that hadn't been picked up, she went to investigate. Perhaps the owners had forgotten to claim them. One wooden box had been jimmied open. Curiosity overcame her reservations. Who would know if she peeked? Kneeling down, she reached inside, and her hand made contact with a hard, irregular object. Pulling it out, she examined it in the last shreds of light and realized it was a carved totem, very much like Quentin's. Flipping it upside down, she noticed a sticker of authenticity like the one she and Eric had seen at the Vancouver art exhibit. What was different about this totem was that it felt heavy, like the genuine article.

Hearing a noise, Wendy dropped the totem back into the crate and swung around, feeling guilty for prying into someone else's belongings.

"Wendy, is that you?" Although she only saw a silhouette in the darkness, she recognized Joe's voice. He came toward her.

"Joe, what are you doing here?" she asked. "Is there an emergency at the hospital?"

"No, no, Connie sent me to find you. She said you wanted to see me."

Something in his voice sent shivers down her spine. What was Connie up to now? "I think she's playing games with you, Joe. I haven't seen Connie since this morning when she relieved me at work. So why don't we just go head over to work together?"

Instead of retreating, Joe moved even closer—much too close. As Wendy tried to walk around him, his arms closed like a vise around her. "Joe!" she cried out.

"I followed you down here, Wendy. I had to talk to you. Please, don't push me away." His breath reeked of alcohol. She struggled against him, which only tightened his grip.

"Joe, let's go to the hospital and talk," she said, trying to sound calm and reasonable. Suddenly she wished she hadn't strolled down to the dark, deserted marina tonight. She struggled to free herself. "Please, let me go. You're hurting me."

"Wendy, I need you. I've wanted you ever since you came here. I thought once Ellerslie left town, you'd turn to me, but instead you threw yourself at Tremaine. I can't stand it anymore." His grip tightened.

Joe was beginning to really scare her. Forcing herself to remain perfectly still, she said quietly but firmly, "Joe, you're a fine doctor, but I don't have those kinds of feelings for you."

"I saw the way you looked at me when we delivered that Whitefoot baby. You and I make a good team, Wendy." He tried to kiss her, but she managed to avert her face in time. Fear turned on her adrenaline, and with a herculean effort she managed to wrench herself free of him and run along the dock.

She could hear him in pursuit of her, and she ran faster. He gained on her enough to grab her jacket hood and bring her to a sudden halt. He swiveled her around. She pushed at him and threw useless punches into the air, which he blocked as if he were swatting a fly. Unexpectedly her fist connected with his chest. It gave him pause, but before she could even think of running, he recovered, and angry now, he shoved her to the ground.

The thought flitted through her dazed mind that since she was already in position, a prayer couldn't hurt. But before she had time to put a coherent thought together, someone rushed past her and plowed into Joe, knocking him off his feet. After a brief scuffle, one figure lay on the ground; the other stood up and turned toward her. Slowly, Wendy rose to her feet, her heart thumping.

"Wendy, are you all right? Did he hurt you?"

Eric! Her breath escaped in a long sigh, and the tension abruptly left her body. Eric drew her into his arms, and she leaned into his quiet strength. It reminded her of their first meeting. He had held her just like this.

She felt his heart pounding as he cradled her against his chest. How could one man's touch—Joe's—generate distaste and fear, while another's sparked a sense of safety and security?

"I was looking for you," Eric said in a calm voice. "Janet told me you'd probably wander in this general direction. I heard you cry out, so I ran."

"Thank you for coming," she said, releasing her tight grip on him. "I'm fine now."

He dropped his arms the minute she loosened her hold and stepped back. "You're welcome," he said with a gentle half smile.

After a moment, she said, "I thought you were with Connie."

He pulled back a little to look at her. "Connie? What gave you that idea?"

Wendy shrugged sheepishly. "I saw you two walking together the other night, and this morning Connie told me she had a date with you this afternoon."

Eric pulled her close again, holding her gently. Against her hair he said softly, "Connie came up to me the other night while I was walking—alone—and asked me about hospitals in the Seattle area. Then she called me yesterday and asked me to meet her today to ask some more questions. That's the extent of our 'date.'"

Wendy shivered.

"I hoped to see *you* tonight," he said, "but not under these circumstances. We need to talk, Wendy, but not now, not here. Shall we go?"

She nodded against his chest. "What about Joe?" She pointed to the man lying motionless in a heap. "He's hurt. . . ." But she couldn't make herself go near him.

"He's drunk. I'll send the police to pick him up," Eric said coldly. "If he needs medical attention, they can take him to the hospital. But I didn't do a lot of damage to him, much as I would have liked to."

"Let's just get out of here," she said, her voice stronger now.

Headlights threw a spotlight on them as a car drove slowly

down the road toward them. It stopped short of the dock, and the driver got out. He walked right up to them.

"Could you two come with me, please?" It was not a request.

"What do you want now, Ganzer?" Eric asked wearily, turning around.

"I would like to speak to you both privately, if you don't mind. My car?"

Chapter Fourteen

Joe moaned.

"Who's that? What's going on here?" Ganzer asked, looking around.

"That's Dr. Chandler, and you're a little late. He tried to force himself on Wendy, and now he's lying over there." Eric pointed vaguely in the direction of the noise. Joe stirred and groaned again.

"Is that true?" the Mountie asked.

Wendy nodded and began to shiver.

"She's in shock, Ganzer. I need to get her out of here."

Ganzer was already kneeling beside the doctor. Joe half sat up, holding his head. He whimpered pitifully.

"He'll live," Ganzer announced, in a tone suggesting it didn't matter either way to him. "I'll take the lot of you with me." The Mountie pulled Joe up as if he weighed nothing and dragged him to the police cruiser parked on the dock. Opening the back door, he pushed him inside. Eric guided Wendy around to the front passenger door, helped her in, and then slipped in beside her.

Ganzer studied Wendy. "Are you all right, Miss Hunt?"

She nodded, unable to look at either man. Shame, humiliation, and a sense of unaccustomed helplessness overwhelmed her. She just wanted to go home, take a long, hot bath, and scrub herself till she could feel clean again.

At the hospital ER, Janet took one look at Joe and immediately called Dr. Thomas.

Joe was conscious but holding his nose. It had bled all over his jacket and now looked like a swollen red bulb on his face. Constable Ganzer helped him stagger to a nearby wheelchair, and he plopped into it. "Sorry, Wendy . . . couldn't help it . . . need you . . . so . . ."

Wendy was stunned. His apology was ludicrous in light of his actions. Janet whisked the injured doctor to Radiology to prepare him for the X-rays Dr. Thomas ordered. When she returned to the emergency room, she looked from Wendy to John Ganzer. "What happened?"

Wendy laughed—a brittle, hollow laugh. "Joe decided to press his attentions a little too aggressively, and Eric showed up just in the nick of time. My hero—again. That makes two rescues, if you're keeping track." Dr. Thomas joined them then, and his hearty manner helped restore Wendy's sense of normalcy. "How is Joe?" she asked him.

"Apart from a broken nose, fine. His alcohol level is keeping him pretty well anesthetized." Shaking his head sadly, the doctor said, "I'm afraid I underestimated his persistence, though, my dear. He won't be working here—or, likely, anywhere—again until he deals with his . . . issues." He patted Wendy's shoulder. "Don't worry, I'll see that he gets help—in Vancouver. The good news is that Dr. Barton is on his way back to us, so we have reinforcements."

Eric was pacing impatiently when she returned to the front desk. "Are you all right?" he instantly asked her. He stood still, but his eyes roamed her face and then proceeded to give the rest of her a thorough inspection.

She nodded, embarrassed at his scrutiny. "I'm fine, thanks to you—" she began, but John Ganzer cut in.

"If you're up to it, I'd still like to talk to you both," he said, his broad shoulders filling the doorway.

"Why don't you just talk to me?" Eric said. "Wendy's been through enough tonight."

Wendy would rather have just gone to bed, but she knew she dared not. She wouldn't want to get up in two hours. Besides, she was burning with curiosity about what Ganzer had to say. "No, I'm fine, really," she assured both men. "And I can't wait to hear what you want to talk about," she added with a sarcastic bite.

Ganzer headed to his police car and waited for them.

"I don't trust him," Wendy whispered to Eric before she remembered that she didn't exactly trust *him,* either.

"I gather you trust *me* a little more, to say that to me. I hope you can trust me a little longer, Wendy."

"Janet said you aren't the lying kind, and I trust *her,*" she retorted, and marched ahead of him. She heard Eric's laughter behind her, and somehow it comforted her immensely. Maybe there was still hope for . . . for whatever could be with Eric.

Ganzer held the passenger door open for Wendy and nodded for Eric to get in the back. "Buckle up," he told them. "We're taking a ride." When they were all buckled in, the Mountie drove off.

"What's going to happen to Joe?" Wendy asked.

"Dr. Thomas will patch him up, and then I'll put him in jail."

Wendy gulped. The man sounded so cold, so heartless. Did he get that way being a Mountie, or had he always been like that?

He glanced at Wendy. "Don't tell me you feel sorry for that jerk."

"That's it, Ganzer," Eric interrupted, leaning forward. "You did your job, and we're grateful. Now, what's all this cloak-and-dagger for?"

The Mountie drove north, out of Shadow Ridge and up the coast until they came to a small diner. Wendy had never been there before. Ganzer parked the car and waved them out. Wendy and Eric followed him into the restaurant. A bell tinkled at their entrance.

One young couple occupied a booth, and two middle-aged men were sitting at the counter, several stools apart. Ganzer chose the booth farthest from the door and sat facing the room. Wendy and Eric sat opposite him.

"So, what's all this about, Constable?" repeated Eric as soon as they sat down.

"First of all, I'll ask the questions," the constable said in a low, authoritative voice. "And you will keep your voices down."

The waitress came with a pot of coffee and three menus.

"Just the coffee, ma'am," Ganzer said with a disarming smile. Wendy was surprised at how deceptively human it made him look. The girl smiled back invitingly. She poured them all coffee, kept the menus, and walked away.

Wendy sipped her coffee and waited.

Ganzer leaned forward, his hands clasped in front of him, and spoke in a low rumble. "What I am about to tell you must remain among only the three of us. As it is, I'm putting my butt on the line to even tell you, but you're charging into our year-long investigation of a smuggling ring, and if I don't stop you, you just may blow the whole thing to pieces. So listen closely—I'm not going to say this twice."

Wendy fought to suppress a smile. The man was dead serious, even though he sounded like something out of an old cop show.

"There's a place on the Queen Charlotte Islands known by the Haida natives as Slate Mountain. They mine a unique black argillite rock there. A totem made from this rock sells for a pretty penny here in Canada. In the States and overseas, it's out of this world. Am I boring you, Miss Hunt?"

Wendy stifled an uncontrollable yawn. After the earlier excitement, her body seemed to simply be shutting down. It was all she could do to keep her eyes open. Even Eric's presence beside her, which usually was enough to set her nerves ablaze, wasn't helping.

"We learned all this from Quentin Whitefoot," Eric explained, putting his arm protectively around Wendy's shoulders. "Do you think we can get to the bottom line, here? Wendy can't last much longer."

"I'm okay, Constable. Go on," she urged.

"All right, Miss Hunt. I'll make it brief. Native carvers make their money selling totems and other knickknacks, mostly in Vancouver. Apparently somebody besides them has tapped into Slate Mountain and has been mining and selling argillite illegally, and the Haidas are furious."

"How can a mountain belong to one tribe?" Wendy inquired.

"It's on Haida land. It's theirs, fair and square," replied Ganzer.

"How can they tell that someone else is mining the mountain, not just other Haida carvers?" Eric asked.

"Good question, Tremaine. It's because only two or three chiefs even know the location of the mine, and all of them agree that huge chunks of argillite have been mined by persons unknown. They asked us to investigate, since the argillite is their bread and butter."

"So, you know that Haida argillite is being smuggled off the Islands," Eric said thoughtfully. After a pause, he said, "I'd guess it's being shipped out to other native carvers, who pay big bucks to get it and then sell their carvings out of the country and make even bigger bucks. Close?"

Ganzer nodded approvingly. "Good guess. Except that it's not being shipped directly from the Islands. It comes here to Shadow Ridge and is secretly stored at the old sawmill."

"So Horace ran into the smugglers? Is that how he ended up in the ravine?" Eric asked, thinking about Scott's similar "accident."

Ganzer shrugged. "Probably. How he got wind of anything going on at the sawmill is a mystery to me. He must be pretty resourceful. As far as anyone in Shadow Ridge is concerned, that mill hasn't been used for ten years or more. Anyway, from the sawmill storehouse, the smugglers ship what their customers order to carve their totems. Finished works are then sent back here for redistribution elsewhere. Shadow Ridge is like the hub of a wheel, with spokes going in and out. . . . Yes, Miss Hunt?"

"There was a crate at the end of the dock this evening. It was filled with argillite totems—real ones. Did you know it was there?" In her tired state, Wendy's reactions were too slow. She should have kept her mouth shut. If Ganzer knew about it, he could easily be one of the smugglers. Hadn't Claude LeBoeuf told them *he* was the RCMP's special agent investigating police corruption and smuggling? Knowing she had seen the crate of totems, Ganzer now probably had to eliminate her—and Eric. They would never make it back to Shadow Ridge. Ten years from now their skeletons would wash up on some remote shore. . . .

Eric shook her awake.

". . . when I came down to the dock to pick it up," Ganzer was saying. "But imagine my surprise to see you two—no, three—there. By the way, exactly why were you there, Miss Hunt?"

Wendy blushed. She would rot in jail before admitting in front of Eric that she had been wandering the town, hoping to run into him. "I . . . uh, was, uh, just taking a walk. I've been on graveyard shift all week, and I wanted to get out for some air." Her voice trailed off.

Ganzer cracked a rare smile. "It's still legal to go for a walk, Miss Hunt. You don't have to sound so guilty. Was Dr. Chandler already there when you arrived, or did he come later?"

"Later," she whispered, beginning to relive her revulsion. "He said he followed me there."

"And he came at you, just like that?"

Eric sat forward, bristling. "What are you suggesting, Ganzer?"

"Nothing," he said blandly. "Just trying to get her statement about the incident. I may as well, while we're talking. Are you ready now, Miss Hunt?"

She nodded and looked him in the eye. "Yes."

"Good. Just tell me in your own words what happened at the dock." His coldness had vanished, and he sounded surprisingly compassionate. *He must get this a lot,* Wendy thought, suddenly realizing that most of what he saw of people was their worst. She felt a pang of sympathy for the man.

"I was on the dock when Joe showed up." She paused to collect her thoughts. "He . . . well, I think he'd been drinking. Anyway, he tried to kiss me and wouldn't take no for an answer. When I tried to get away, he grabbed me, and I fought him off. I ended up punching him pretty hard, and that made him furious. He shoved me. And then suddenly Eric appeared and saved the day."

Ganzer had been taking notes, and when she finished, he put away his pad and pen. "That's it?"

Wendy nodded.

"Okay. I'll have this typed up tomorrow, and you can come to the station and sign it."

And that was that. Weariness wrapped around Wendy like a shroud, dulling her senses. She wished she didn't have to work that night, but knew someone would have to pull a double shift if she failed to turn up. Besides, the hospital probably was not too busy.

"Are we finished here, Ganzer?" Eric asked, looking pointedly at Wendy's vacant stare.

"I certainly hope you're finished," Ganzer replied. "Finished interfering, that is. We are just about to put the whole smuggling operation to bed—we're that close. You are putting yourself into extreme danger with your amateurish mucking around and asking questions about your brother. You could be undoing a year's worth of work here. Scott Ellerslie stumbled around just like you're doing, Tremaine. Take head of that, and stay out of this."

Eric leaned close to Ganzer. "What did happen to Scott?"

"I can't say. In fact, I warned him, just like I am you. Whatever happened to Ellerslie was his own fault."

Eric sat back, shaking his head.

"Scott was a big boy, Tremaine. He knew he was getting in over his head. He was sure he could handle it."

"You know, Constable," Wendy observed, "you're not exactly the soul of tact."

Ganzer stared at her. "I couldn't care less what you think I am or am not, Miss Hunt. But if you and Tremaine don't stay out of my way, I will most definitely put you both in jail without a moment's hesitation. In fact, it will be my pleasure. Is that clear?" He didn't wait for a response. Leaving a few bills on the table for the coffee, he indicated the door. They had no choice but to go with him. He had the car.

Ganzer drove to the nurses' residence first. Something had been bothering Wendy all the way home. As soon as Ganzer stopped the car in front of the dorm, she asked, "What part does Constable LeBoeuf play in your investigation, Constable Ganzer? He suggested that he's investigating *you*. Maybe you should get your stories straight, eh?"

She opened her door to make a quick exit, but Ganzer's voice stopped her. "Stay away from Claude LeBoeuf, Miss Hunt, if you know what's good for you. He can be a very dangerous adversary."

Wendy had never been so glad to see her tiny bedroom. Her body ached all over. She jumped into a hot shower and let the heat soothe away the soreness. She tried not to think about anything except how good the hot water felt. She had no idea anymore who was telling the truth. She thought Eric knew more about this whole mess, but since he wasn't talking, there was nothing she could do.

The water turned cold, and reluctantly Wendy left the shower. When she surveyed herself in the mirror, she saw a bruise on her arm, and by the time she was dressed, her head and neck were aching. She was grateful she would have the next three days off. Slipping into her jacket, she went down the hill to the hospital.

An hour later, Eric came by to check on her. At least Ganzer hadn't roughed him up or anything after her comments about the two Mounties getting their stories straight. Her relief that nothing had come of her stupid remark might have explained her unusual behavior: she threw her arms around Eric and buried her head in his chest. Or maybe she was suffering from post-traumatic stress disorder. Yes, that sounded much better.

"You're still a little shaky, aren't you?" Eric said as he removed her arms from around his waist and stepped away from her. "Don't worry. Chandler's locked up. He can't hurt you," he said reassuringly. "I just don't understand why they still made you work tonight."

"They didn't. I wouldn't sleep very well anyway. Better to be doing something useful if I'm going to be awake. What did you make of John Ganzer's revelations?"

Eric didn't quite make eye contact. "I think he's right," he said evasively. "We should cease and desist our attempts at detective work. For all we know, both Ganzer and LeBoeuf might be lying. Maybe Corporal Standish is our white knight."

He said it half-jokingly, but Wendy nodded thoughtfully. "Standish certainly is the least likely to be a special investigator with the RCMP, isn't he? Therefore, he must be it."

"I don't think it really works that way," Eric said, his crooked grin sending delicious sensations through her whole body. She couldn't help an answering smile from spreading across her face. Tension instantly sprang up between them.

"I wish you'd stop looking at me that way," Eric murmured. Slowly, with infinite gentleness, he pulled her close and held her against his chest. Wendy rested there, feeling safe and cherished, lulled by the steady drumbeat of his heart. As his hands gently stroked her back, she burrowed closer. His breathing quickened. She groaned softly.

Abruptly he pushed her away. "Wendy, I . . . I shouldn't take advantage of you this way. I'm sorry."

Disappointed and hurt, Wendy withdrew, trying to look unconcerned at his abrupt change in mood.

Eric's face gave nothing away as he backed away. "You'll understand very soon. All will become clear, I promise." He left without another word.

Another promise. Wendy hated promises.

Chapter Fifteen

As the night hours crept away, Wendy thought long and hard about Eric's promise. She felt sure he was withholding something important. It had to be important, or it wouldn't have created such a chasm between them. Her brain was fuzzy with fatigue by the time the morning shift arrived to relieve her. She went straight home and fell into bed, exhausted.

Several hours later, a loud crash catapulted Wendy out of her deep sleep. "Well, I guess I'll get up now," she muttered crossly, wide awake, feet on the floor. As her ears registered the assorted bumps and thumps echoing all through the residence, memory returned. The hospital's Spring Social was tonight. Dressing quickly, she ran downstairs to see how things were progressing. With the glow of Eric's warm embrace carrying her two inches off the ground, she again allowed herself the luxury of hope. Tonight she would see him, maybe dance with him, even wheedle the truth out of him.

The withdrawal she had sensed from him after he had talked with John Ganzer was gone for a few moments last night. But it had returned all too quickly. He had promised she would know everything very soon, and despite his recent coolness, she hoped he would keep that promise. She had learned to distrust men's promises, but this man, she reminded herself, was different from most men. Even Janet had told her so, and she was counting on Janet's expert verdict to be correct.

Connie, just coming off her shift, walked in. With a brittle smile, she nodded, barely acknowledging Wendy, then went upstairs. What about Connie and Eric? Wendy wanted to believe Eric's explanation, but could she? Something caught her thoughts up short. It was the memory of her Aunt Lily's words about her mother's doubts destroying her father's love. If her mother had only been able to trust her husband, would their marriage have succeeded? Had her mother's fears become self-fulfilling prophecies? At this moment, Wendy wished with all her heart that she could talk to her father. Never before had she questioned the wisdom of taking the negative road, the road of doubts, fears, and mistrust. She had always thought that was the smart thing to do. But it had ended in bitter loneliness for her mother. Was that the future Wendy wanted?

All afternoon, she kept busy helping wherever there was a need. As the partygoers began arriving, Wendy realized she was hungry. Keeping one eye on the entrance for a glimpse of Eric, she nibbled sandwiches while passing around trays. Then she helped foursomes team up for bridge and other card games at the tables that had been set up. She had been forewarned to keep Mrs. Katz and Mr. Blunt at different tables, and when she saw them both gravitate toward the same table, she rushed in to divert Mrs. Katz to a table with less aggressive players.

As she looked up, Eric walked through the door. With studied nonchalance, she made her way toward the punch table, hoping he would head there first. *Why not just crawl over to him and beg?* her mother seemed to whisper. Wendy shook off the thought. She loved Eric. He was worth fighting her fears for. Her mother's voice had lost a little power.

Eric's progress across the room came to a halt when Shirley

waylaid him. As always, Eric was polite and charming, and Shirley was lapping it up. A pang of pure, gut-piercing jealousy stabbed Wendy right in her midsection. Her mother's words gained the upper hand for that moment.

Shirley drifted away, and Wendy made herself useful at the punch table by filling several glasses. In two seconds, she decided, if Eric didn't come to her, she was going to take the mountain—in this case, a glass of punch—to him.

"He can't last long without something to drink," she muttered, pouring another glass.

"And you're not crazy because you talk to yourself," said a husky male voice beside her.

"Constable LeBoeuf!" Flustered at his sudden appearance, Wendy stammered. She held out the glass. "Punch?"

He smiled, and at that moment Wendy knew why he had no trouble finding a date every Saturday night, even in a town with few available females. His hooded eyes and the way they looked intently into hers were potent.

"How come you're not dancing, pretty thing?" Claude looked very dashing in a dark V-neck sweater over black trousers. "I will have that punch," he said, caressing her fingers as he took it from her.

"Bien sûr, mon ami," she said.

His eyebrows shot up. *"Tu parle français, ma petite?"* He laughed, and she felt sure he practiced that laugh in front of the mirror—a lot. He had a wonderful set of teeth and a perfect, husky laugh. Had Eric seen them together? She could only hope.

Wendy shook her head. "Not really. I just did that to sound impressive. Did I say it wrong?"

"Well, calling someone *ami* in French *can* imply more than friendship, if you know what I mean."

There was no mistaking what LeBoeuf meant. Wendy glanced over to see if Eric was watching them right now, because she certainly didn't want him to miss any of Claude's seductive moves.

"I didn't know," she said. "That's not what I mean—"

He took her hand and pulled her close to his side. "Perhaps we can make it true. Dance with me, *cherie*," he said, and he twirled her around and into his arms.

Wendy looked around for Eric, but he had disappeared from view. *Shoot! All this for nothing.*

She had no desire to dance with the Mountie and tried to keep her distance from him, but with great finesse he maneuvered her close, cradling her right hand lovingly against his broad chest, while keeping a hand firmly at her back. She could barely tolerate his touch, and as soon as the music stopped, she pulled away from him. "Thank you for the dance, *monsieur,* but I must go and pass out another plate of sandwiches," Wendy said, anxious to leave his presence. "I'm sure you have more important things to do than stay here and dance with me. Good night." She started to walk away, but the music began again, and he pulled her back into his arms.

"*Cherie,* I have nothing more important—" He glanced at his wristwatch. "At least not for another hour. You're too pretty to be left alone. Come, just one more dance."

"Well, one more. Then I must circulate and be available. . . ."

He pulled her into his arms. "So, what did you and Tremaine discuss with Ganzer last night?" he asked casually.

"How did you know . . . ?" she stammered, immediately on her guard. She gave up all pretense of dancing, and he let her go. They strolled over to the punch table, and she went through the motions of filling glasses. Wendy scanned the room for a glimpse of Eric, but he was nowhere in sight. Something was wrong. She could feel it.

LeBoeuf persisted. "I know everything that goes on here, Wendy. Did you tell Ganzer about my undercover work?" He spoke in a low voice so they wouldn't be overheard, but low as it was, it carried a veiled threat that made Wendy's pulse begin to thump erratically. John Ganzer's words about Claude LeBoeuf's being a dangerous adversary sprang to her mind.

"As a matter of fact, we talked about me and about Eric's brother, mostly."

He nodded, "So you didn't mention seeing me in Vancouver?"

Wendy was a terrible liar. Whenever she tried to tell a fib, she turned red from the neck up and broke out in a cold sweat. "I don't believe it ever came up, no," she said, grateful that that was true.

LeBoeuf seemed to relax. "Whatever happened to that friend of Tremaine's—Horatio, or something like that?"

"Horace," supplied Wendy automatically.

"And where is he now?" LeBoeuf was surveying the crowd as if unconcerned about her answer, as if he were just making polite conversation, but she had the distinct impression that he was more interested in Horace's whereabouts than his behavior indicated.

"Eric sent him back to Washington."

"So he recovered, did he? Did he remember who pushed him into the ravine?"

Those words triggered something in Wendy's mind—a memory of Claude LeBoeuf in a tattered trench coat, sitting at the table in the Vancouver restaurant, saying, *Whoever sent Ellerslie over that cliff* . . . She realized that most of the people in town thought Scott Ellerslie had simply packed up and moved on. Only two people knew what had really happened— Quentin . . . and the person who had been there arguing with Scott that night. The person who had pushed him over the cliff. *Claude LeBoeuf!*

Slowly, she backed away from the grinning constable.

"You are not just beautiful, *ma chere,* but very clever *aussi.* I can see in your face that you have figured things out enough to be dangerous to me. Come with me, *s'il vous plaît,*" LeBoeuf ordered in a tone quite different from a moment ago, gripping her arm.

Wendy looked frantically around for Eric, but he was nowhere in sight.

Just then, Mrs. Jarvis came up to the table for a glass of punch. Wendy seized the opportunity to elude LeBoeuf's grasp. Surely he would not do anything in front of all these people. But where was Eric? Hadn't she seen him talking to John Ganzer only moments ago?

"Wendy, can you play a fourth hand here?" called Mr. Henry from nearby. She stumbled and nearly sat on his lap in her haste, but Claude grabbed her arm so tightly it hurt.

"Sorry, sir, I need to steal Wendy away for a private moment. You understand, I'm sure," he said with a wink and an oily smile. He pulled her along, whispering in her ear, "If you so much as raise your voice, I'll have your friend Eric killed instantly."

"You have him?" she gasped. Her surprise and fear made his job easier.

"You don't see him, do you?" Within seconds they had reached the front door, and LeBoeuf forced her out.

The next few minutes passed in a blur. As soon as Wendy cleared the steps, someone grabbed her arm and yanked her away from the constable. The next thing she saw was Claude LeBoeuf lying in a heap at the bottom of the steps, with John Ganzer standing like a colossus above him.

"It's all over, Claude," Ganzer said. "We've picked up your men at the rendezvous point. I have to tell you, there is no loyalty among thieves. They're spilling their guts right now about your operation." He pulled LeBoeuf to his feet, handcuffed him, and led him to the waiting police car.

"Are you all right, Miss Hunt?" said the man holding her arm. It took her a second to place that voice. She turned to find Corporal Standish beside her. "You were very brave just now, and calm, considering you must have been terrified." Somehow he sounded different from the last time they had met, more professional.

"Thanks," she said, unable to think of anything else. Her mind was trying to process what had just happened. "Where's Eric?" she asked. "Claude said he had Eric, that he would kill him if I didn't go with him."

Despite all the pronouns, Standish seemed to know exactly what she was talking about. He shook his head. "Tremaine's fine. He's been with us all along. He said he would meet you at Meg's Café at nine tomorrow morning. Something about a surprise for you." Then he joined John Ganzer in the police car, and they drove off, leaving Wendy to speculate about Eric's surprise.

It occurred to her that she had come a long way in her trust issues when one of her wildest guesses involved an engagement ring or a proposal of marriage. Unlikely as that was, she could hardly wait for morning.

Chapter Sixteen

Wendy walked into Meg's Café early. She had been awake since seven, watching the minutes tick by. At last, unable to contain her excitement, she had rushed over to Meg's at 8:30. She was not alone in her haste to arrive.

Eric stood up, his crooked grin firmly in place. "I had a feeling you'd be early," he said. "I ordered the Workman's Breakfast especially for you."

"Eric, I'm so glad you're okay!" she said. Before she could give him a hug, he put a hand out to forestall her. Now she could see that his smile was merely for show. His eyes told another story. He looked . . . closed off. It was as if *he* had put up a no-trespassing sign. How ironic. So this was what if felt like. Poor Joe.

"Turn around, Wendy," Eric said, looking behind her. She turned, and he said, "Surprise!"

A man stood up from another table and approached her. He walked with a noticeable limp, and shadows hid his face. But as soon as he said, "Hey there, remember me?" she knew.

"Scott!" she cried, and she threw her arms around his neck,

holding him tightly. He welcomed her hug and returned it with enthusiasm. She pulled back to study his face and then hugged him again.

"Hey, hey, careful of the mending ribs." He laughed, giving her one last squeeze before breaking the connection. "Am I glad to see you again, Wendy. I don't mind telling you there were moments when I wondered if I ever would." He sounded older. "Eric tells me you didn't give up trying to find me."

She barely heard him; she kept touching him to make sure he was real. "Scott, you're alive!" she exclaimed happily. "But how . . . ? Where have you been?"

Scott laughed. "I was hoping you'd be surprised to see me. I swore Eric to secrecy."

Wendy's hands stopped moving. "Eric knew you were all right? Since when?"

"Since last week." He laughed at Wendy's grim expression. "Uh-oh. I think I've gotten him into deep doo-doo." Scott took her elbow and began walking back to his table.

"You're limping," she said, taking his arm as if he were a patient. "Shouldn't you be in bed or something?" He sat down and extended his hand to indicate that she sit as well. "I've been in bed long enough, darlin'. I need exercise, or I'll get fat."

"Hardly. In fact, you need some flesh on those bones, mister." His gaunt frame and pallor worried her. So many questions buzzed around her head that she hardly knew which one to ask first.

The café door opened to admit John Ganzer. He glanced around the room and with an air of purpose came directly to Scott's table, extended his hand, and said, "Well done, Ellerslie. You paid quite a price, but I think you'll find it worth it. There'll be a citizen's medal in this for you."

Scott shook the constable's hand and beamed. "Wow. Did you hear that, Wendy? A medal."

"That's great, Scott. Congratulations." Obviously, despite his trials, Scott had not lost his endearing zest for life that had drawn her to him. But as curious as Wendy was to hear his story, she couldn't help but notice that Eric had not joined them at the table. In fact, after reuniting Wendy and Scott, he seemed to have made a discreet withdrawal.

Then she spotted him out the window, walking toward the motel. It occurred to her sadly that now that Scott was safe, Eric's mission in Shadow Ridge was over. At one time, she had been a "distraction" from it. And lately Eric had seemed so distant, she wondered whether he even remembered their shared kisses—kisses that had stormed the gates of her heart.

She forced herself to focus on the man of the hour sitting beside her, gazing at her with an odd expression. "So you were working with the Mounties all along, Scott?" she asked with a modicum of enthusiasm she had dredged up from somewhere.

"Originally Scott came here to do an article on native art," John Ganzer said with less than his usual detachment. In fact, Wendy would have described him as almost animated. "We recruited him with the offer of a much more interesting story— about smuggling."

"Unfortunately, I wasn't a great undercover man," Scott said with a sheepish grin. "Claude LeBoeuf got suspicious and decided to get rid of me."

Meg had brought over two breakfast plates, the same kind Eric and Wendy had enjoyed—a long time ago, it seemed. She couldn't eat a bite. As Scott tucked a large napkin over his shirtfront, she said, "Did Claude LeBoeuf actually push you over the cliff?"

"No, he was about to shoot me, and I figured I'd have better odds if I jumped and rolled down the embankment."

Wendy watched Scott shove a piece of bacon into his mouth with gusto. "Quentin heard you fall," she said. "It's a wonder you didn't end up with a broken neck."

"Someone was watching over me, all right," Scott said, using his fork to point upward.

"How on earth did you disappear in the twenty minutes it took Quentin to get help?"

This time the Mountie answered for Scott, who was making swift inroads into the huge meal. "We had given Scott a GPS device. His fall activated an alarm signal that led me straight to him. I brought him to Dr. Barton's home. We couldn't let LeBoeuf know that Scott was still alive, so as soon as we could, we got the good doctor and Scott off to Vancouver on an RCMP plane."

"Dr. Barton!" Wendy exclaimed. "That explains his sudden leave."

"And John Ganzer spread the story that I'd left town," Scott added. He took a large gulp of orange juice to wash down his hash browns. Wendy felt a bit queasy. "The Mountie plane whisked me to Vancouver General, and I just got out of their off-site rehab center last week."

"Why couldn't someone let us know you were all right?" Wendy cast an accusing glance at John Ganzer.

"You didn't even know he was missing till Tremaine showed up looking for him," Ganzer reminded her. "Besides, we couldn't afford to tip off LeBoeuf. He had to believe that Scott was either dead or too incapacitated to tell his story. As it was, I had to confide in Tremaine so he wouldn't mess up our carefully laid trap." Ganzer stood up. "Don't be too upset with him, Miss Hunt. I threatened to throw him in jail if he breathed a word to you. In my experience, women are not the best secret keepers."

Wendy frowned at his sexist remark, but the personal tidbit about himself piqued her curiosity. She must remember to ask Janet about it.

"I've got to get back, Ellerslie," the Mountie said. "You can fill your girlfriend in on the rest of your heroics." He bestowed a rare smile on both of them. "You'll be hearing from us." As he left the café, a bell tinkled when the door opened and closed.

Wendy watched Scott clean up his plate and pour himself a cup of coffee from the carafe Meg had brought. He added his usual three sugars and a dollop of cream before she said as casually as she could, "Where did Eric go?"

"Probably back to the motel to pack," Scott told her without looking at her. When she said nothing, he looked up. His expression was unreadable. Putting down his empty cup and crumpling his napkin, he threw it onto his empty plate and said abruptly, "Let's get out of here. I need to walk a bit, or I get stiff."

They left the café, and Scott stumbled on the sidewalk's uneven pavement. "Blast!" Instantly, Wendy reached out to help him, taking his arm to lend him support. Scott winced. "I'm okay. Just not quite back there yet," he said, his scrunched-up face revealing his pain.

"I've got you," she assured him. "Lean on me."

"I think I did that a lot when I was first here, sweetheart. It's time I stood on my own two feet." He took a breath and grinned at her through clenched teeth. "I'm okay now. Let's keep going."

Scott turned in the direction of the Raven Motel. "Walk me to the Raven, would you, Wendy? You can say good-bye to Eric," he added.

With a hollow feeling in the pit of her stomach, she whispered, "He's leaving? I mean, both of you are leaving? When?"

"Today. Eric made the reservations. Go figure. Leaving this beautiful spot and all." Scott's quick glance made Wendy feel uneasy, but she was not sure why. "The only excuse I can give for the guy is that he's never been in love before, and he doesn't know how to handle it. Or he's just plain stupid."

"He's not stupid. He's in love?" *Connie!* If it were possible, Wendy felt even worse. "With whom?"

Scott laughed. "I see he's met his match. With you, silly—who else? As soon as he found out I was safe, he started in on me about having put you into danger. I have to say that from my perspective, *I* was clearly the one in danger, and *he* was the one who roped you into the whole mess, but he insists it's my fault." Scott looked at Wendy with an innocent face. "Doesn't that tell you how screwy his thinking is? So, as glad as I am to see him again, I'm contemplating another road trip if you can't straighten him out."

"Don't joke about that, Scott. Eric needs your forgiveness for driving you away; he needs you." Wendy fastened on the one thing Scott had said that she could handle. The rest was too much to hope for.

"Don't worry, Wendy—forgiveness already asked for and given. Facing death puts your life into a different perspective. Over the last several weeks I've had a lot of time to think. For a while it was up in the air if I would have the use of both legs again."

He smiled at Wendy's sympathetic protest.

For the first time she saw the resemblance between Eric and Scott, amazed that she had never seen it before. Of all things, they had the same killer smile.

"My brother and I hashed out a lot of things," he continued, "and I have a feeling you had a lot to do with Eric's recent mellowness." He patted her on the back and then added, "But one thing puzzles me. And I think you may have the answer for that."

Wendy couldn't imagine that and said so.

"For some reason Eric is under the impression that you and I are in love." Scott stopped walking and turned her to face him. "Now, how do you suppose he got that idea?"

Chapter Seventeen

Scott and Wendy approached the motel. Fishing the keys to his brother's truck out of a jacket pocket, Scott informed her that he was going to visit Quentin.

"What about your leg? Are you able to drive?"

Hobbling into the vehicle, Scott laughed. "It's only my brake foot that's wonky. I'll be fine." As he started the engine, he added, "You have thirty minutes to straighten my brother out, woman, or else I'll have to do it myself. And it won't be pretty if I do it." He waved and spun gravel as he drove away.

The door to Eric's room was slightly ajar, so she walked in. His back to her, Eric was putting clothes into a suitcase that lay open on one of the beds. Without turning around, he said, "It's about time, little brother. The plane leaves in less than an hour."

Wendy coughed. "Scott took your truck to go see Quentin. He said he'd be back in half an hour."

He spun around. "Wendy!" After a momentary flash of warmth, his expression seemed to shut down. He turned away from her. "Well, then, it won't be long until you see him again."

"I'm not concerned about that right now." She wondered if Scott was playing a joke on her by saying that Eric loved her. Then Wendy remembered the kisses, the tenderness Eric had shown her in Vancouver, his understanding about her father, his sense of humor, and the way he had fought Joe for her honor. But did that add up to love?

Her mother's voice pounded in her head: *Men betray you. Don't trust them.* Wendy heard the mantra, but this time she shook her head and silently shouted back, *No!* Her mother's fears had not only destroyed her own life but also Wendy's chance to grow up with her father's love. It was time to end it, right here, right now. Wendy loved Eric Tremaine with all her heart. Whether he returned that love or whether it had only been "chemistry" to him, she would not let him leave Shadow Ridge until he knew how she felt.

Straightening her spine, she ignored his outward coolness. Having decided to believe what she couldn't see, she said, "As a matter of fact, Scott doesn't concern me as much as you do."

He kept packing. She definitely had an uphill battle. "So, you're leaving." *Wow. Brilliant observation, Wendy.*

"My purpose here is over," Eric said as if he had rehearsed it. "Scott is fine, the mystery is solved, and the bad guys are in jail." *Tick, tick, tick.* He continued rearranging clothes in the suitcase.

"When were you going to say good-bye to me?" she asked, barely above a whisper.

That turned him around to face her, although he didn't quite meet her eyes. "Before I went. I couldn't risk another black mark against me." His tone was light, but his bleak expression made her heart ache.

"Being a hero wipes out all black marks," she said, trying to lighten the mood. "I believe you still have room for a couple of slips."

"Well, I'm glad of that." He went to the bathroom to retrieve his toiletry articles.

Wendy hunted desperately for a way to break through his

barrier. What could she say? Or do? How could she convince him that she loved him? And that she and Scott had never been more to each other than friends?

Eric returned from the bathroom with a small leather bag and a can of shaving cream, which he threw on top of the clothes in the suitcase. He glanced at her, then looked away again. "You and I both know I got you into danger, so I wouldn't exactly call me a hero."

"Eric, would you please look at me?" He looked up. "You saved me from Joe, and we both know that *he* wasn't your fault."

He turned away from her on the pretext of checking the closet for more clothes. They could both see that all his belongings had already been transferred to the suitcase. "You owe me nothing, Wendy."

"Why do you keep pushing me and Scott together? What about our . . . 'chemistry,' yours and mine?"

"What about the way you greeted Scott at the café this morning?" he countered. "I saw plenty of 'chemistry' in that embrace. Since the moment I came to Shadow Ridge, I've heard all about you and Scott—like it was just a matter of time before you two made it official. I came along when you were missing him, and maybe I confused you." He looked at her with an expression she had never seen. "I found it hard to resist . . . our 'chemistry.' But as soon as I knew Scott was alive and coming back, I had to give you two the chance to figure it all out."

She shook her head. "If I allowed you to believe there was something between Scott and me, that was only to protect myself."

Eric said nothing. At least he had stopped pretending to pack and looked more engaged in the discussion.

"Try to keep up with me here, Eric. It's important." She smiled to take any edge off her words. She was gratified to see a smile tugging at his lips. And she loved him for that. "Scott and I got along like a brother and sister. There was absolutely no tension, not an ounce of . . . 'chemistry' between us, just friendship."

He stared hard at her; she could almost see the wheels of calculation spinning in his head. With all that thinking, he must have the mother of all headaches.

At that moment, Wendy took a significant step forward in her struggle to trust. With determination sired by desperation, she closed the gap between them. Putting her arms around his neck, she leaned against his chest and brought her face within inches of his. The experience was not unlike cuddling up to a rock.

"Whether you like it or not, Eric Tremaine, you are the man I want." She whispered it against his lips, hoping her clumsy technique would put her point across, not cause him to burst out laughing. He went absolutely still.

Wendy felt the air seeping out of her balloon of determination. She had shot her bolt of courage. Was she wrong about Eric's feelings? Was Scott simply his excuse for letting her down gently? Mixed emotions choked her as she turned away and headed to the door.

Her movement seemed to bring Eric to life. "Wendy, don't go. Please." She heard him behind her and whipped around. She hardly dared breathe, let alone hope.

"Did you just say . . . ?" he began. The look in his eyes drew her closer. "You're absolutely sure it's not Scott . . . ?" His eyes never left her face. "Because if not . . ." He cocked his head to one side, letting his gaze roam over her. "I'd like to restart this conversation from where you put your arms around me, like this . . ." He demonstrated by putting her arms around his neck. "And then I want to tell you what an idiot I've been to even think of letting you go." He smiled his lopsided, endearing grin. "You're the one I want, too, Wendy Hunt."

What she saw in his eyes made her blush. The barriers were gone, and his love shone through. "Oh, Eric!" She gave him a watery smile. His arms tightened around her, and she needed no further instruction. Molding herself to him, she delighted in the strength of his embrace. And then Eric pulled back, took her face in his hands with exquisite tenderness, and kissed her exactly the way she had dreamed he would.

Some time later, Scott returned to find them locked in a passionate embrace. He laughed as they broke apart hurriedly, and he said, "You know, I figured you two would hit it off a long time ago. Didn't I tell you once that you and Eric were a perfect match, Wendy? Anyway, I just came to warn you that the plane is leaving in fifteen minutes." He glanced at Eric. "My guess is that I'm going back to Rosewood alone, right?"

Eric nodded. "Wendy and I need some time to get to know each other without having to dodge bad guys. And she'll have to give notice at her job." He looked at her questioningly.

She nodded, saying, "As long as we get back here to visit sometimes."

Scott beamed. "Sure thing. I'll go back and get the wedding preparations under way." He winked at Wendy. "And you can count on me to take care of things at the ranch till you get home, Eric. Take as long as you like."

Impulsively, Eric grabbed Scott by the shoulders and pulled him into a quick, brotherly hug. "Thank God I didn't lose you, Scott." Releasing his grip, Eric straightened and coughed, as if embarrassed at his own actions. Giving Scott a brotherly punch on the arm, he added gruffly, "And try not to get ahead of yourself with the wedding preparations, all right? Wendy has some relatives we'll need to round up."

Scott was as visibly moved by his brother's unexpected demonstration of affection as Wendy was by his understated proposal—and his consideration of her job, her parents, and her aunt and uncle. Scott turned bright pink and remarked, "Well, I hope this means there'll be no bloodletting because of the ding in your truck. It's trickier than I thought to drive with one foot."

Wendy caught Eric's eye, wondering if he remembered that the same truck had been a catalyst to their first meeting. He gave her a look so tender she felt the warmth of it spread through her. In his eyes shone the love she had almost missed in her attempts to protect herself. At last she had come out of the shadows of fear and doubt that had shackled her heart for so long. At last, Wendy had come home.